Fury

A Kate Redman Mystery: Book 11

Celina Grace

For my sister in law, Cheryl Beckles
and to the memory of my brother in
law, Mark Beckles, with my love

Author's Note

SOME TIME AGO, ONE OF my readers asked me what Detective Chief Inspector Anderton's first name was. The embarrassing truth was *that I didn't know*. He'd only ever been Anderton for me! But I thought it would be a good thing to ascertain, so I asked my lovely reader team for their suggestions. A big thanks to them all for making so many good suggestions, some bonkers and some absolutely barmy (a special thanks to Thomas King for his suggestion 'Derek Charles Ian', hoho:)) but in the end I went with one from Angela Ferguson, so thank you very much for that, Angela! As for what it is? You'll have to read on and find out ;).

Prologue

THE LEAVES WERE BEGINNING TO fall, lying in rustling piles on the rough surface of the lane that led to Roland Barry's house. They crunched satisfyingly under his shoes as he walked along under the setting sun, an orange orb in a blood-red sky. Very dramatic, thought Roland, who appreciated a good sunset. The outline of the trees on the ridge of the hill stood out like black sentinels. The day had been warm; one of those early autumn days golden with sunshine, but now the night was drawing in, and the faintest whisper of winter carried on the air. Just a touch of chill; enough to make Dr Barry plunge his bare hands into the pockets of his Barbour jacket and hurry a little faster towards home.

His house was the only one to be found down that particular lane. Sometimes, if he didn't leave the house, he wouldn't see anyone other than the postman for days. But today, he'd been for lunch with his sister, and after an afternoon of company (Barbara was a good soul, but she'd always been a talker) he was anticipating a quiet evening in front of the fire. A glass of wine and the new library book he had picked out a few days ago awaited him. Supper on a tray and perhaps a film, if he had the energy.

He kicked through the last of the leaves before he reached the driveway of his house, a small stone cottage surrounded on three sides by lawns and shrubbery. The garden looked a little frowsty. Might do some work on that tomorrow, Roland thought, providing the weather's not too bad. The chill had set in now and he hunched against it as he hurried up the bricked path to the front door. The key seemed to stick a little at first, and he pulled it from the lock, frowning. The second attempt at unlocking the door proved more successful. Roland went inside, shutting the front door behind him, thankful for the warmth of the hallway.

Once inside, Roland paused. Had he heard something upstairs? He listened again but decided it was nothing. This was an old house, full of creaks and whispers. Haunted, probably, but he'd never seen or heard anything in the ten years he'd lived here. Roland had no fear of the supernatural. There was only one thing he feared, and he'd taken many steps to ensure that would never happen.

Frowning again as the memories resurfaced, Roland shook his head and moved towards the living room. He always laid a fire before he went out; he was a methodical man and knew it saved time when one returned at the end of a long day. Wincing at the crack of his arthritic knees, he knelt down and applied a match. As the fire blossomed into red and yellow flowers of warmth, Roland heaved himself back to his feet with a groan and went to switch on the table lamp by his favourite armchair.

Warm light filled the room, and Roland paused. A flicker of anxiety passed through his consciousness, so minute as to almost not be felt. But it *was* felt. He frowned again. There was something wrong with the room. What was it? He let his gaze drift from furniture to walls and floors, past pictures on the walls, and past the piano. What was wrong?

It took him another minute to pinpoint it. Once he'd realised what it was, he stared, feeling that flicker of anxiety grow bigger. Without taking his eyes off it, Roland walked forward. Where the hell had *that* come from?

Amongst the ornaments on the sideboard was a small statue, about six inches high. Looking as though it were carved out of black marble, the statue was of a woman, naked and posed in the classical style, unremarkable except for the wings that grew back from her shoulders. Roland stared, alarmed and puzzled. How had it got there? He knew he had never seen it before in his life. Where had it *come from*?

He was so lost in staring and puzzling that he failed to notice the faint footsteps behind him or the slight whisper of displaced air as someone moved quickly towards him. The thump of something hard and heavy across the back of his knees was the first thing he was aware of, the motion scything his legs out from under him. Roland had time for one quick squawk of distress before he hit the living room floor. His head hit the bottom of the sideboard as he fell, stunning him. For a few moments, he lost consciousness and was unaware of his arms being hauled behind his back, the snap of handcuffs around his wrists and his ankles. Groaning, he began to come around to consciousness just as his assailant hauled him into the centre of the room.

Roland managed to open his eyes. He could feel the warm tickle of blood running down one side of his face. For a confused moment, he thought it was one of the trees on the ridge standing there, a black sentinel, all sharp angles. But as he blinked and groaned, reality hit him. It was a person, black-clad—entirely black-clad. All he could see of their face was a pair of eyes gleaming from behind the mask of a balaclava.

A terrorist. That must be it. Roland remembered all the pictures from the media; the black-clad murderers, their bomb-belts, their guns and their knives. He felt paralysing terror. Was he about to be beheaded? But that didn't make sense. Why would a terrorist be *here*? Why him?

"Please," he croaked, "Don't hurt me. I don't know what you want but please don't hurt me."

His assailant had been standing with both arms behind their back, their feet planted square. Something about their stance recalled the military to Roland. It was the stance of a soldier standing to attention. Was this person a terrorist after all?

The person—he couldn't say whether it was a man or a woman—brought their arms forward. In each hand was an object, one innocuous and one that brought a moan of fear to Roland's lips. The person stepped forward, bringing the photograph and the knife within inches of Roland's face.

Roland had focused on the knife, a wicked six inches of steel with a black rubber handle. It wasn't until the knife was drawn back a little and the photograph thrust into his line of sight that Roland realised what it was.

All the blood seemed to leave his body. Dimly, over the paralysing wash of fear, shock and horror, he felt his bladder go, the warmth of urine flooding over his trousers. In less than a second, upon recognition of the photograph, Roland knew that whatever steps he had taken hadn't been enough. Perhaps they had never been enough.

Those gleaming eyes met his. Roland opened his mouth to gasp, to say 'no' or to beg and plead for his life; he didn't know which. But by that time, the knife was coming down, moving through the air in a shining streak of silver, and by then, it was too late—far too late—to say anything at all.

Chapter One

"Can I get up yet?"

"Not yet. Just give me one more minute."

Anderton's voice sounded as though he was downstairs. Kate Redman rolled her eyes and settled back against the pillows. It was always warm at Anderton's place, and Kate was grateful for the warmth, especially this morning. Whilst the autumn days were warm, the mornings and evenings heralded the promise of the chill soon to come.

There were the sound of footsteps on the stairs and the chink of china and glass. Kate, pretty sure of what was about to happen, pinned an expectant smile on her face. Not that she wasn't pleased – breakfast in bed was always a treat.

"Ta-da!" Anderton pushed the bedroom door open with one foot and manoeuvred himself through, juggling a tray loaded with dishes and cups, a newspaper clutched under one arm. As he successfully fitted himself into the small space at the end of the bed, the paper crashed to the floor in a flurry of pages. Anderton nearly dropped the tray.

"Bugger—"

"Let me help." Kate was already pushing back the duvet.

"No, no. I insist. Come on, Detective Inspector Redman. Sit back and enjoy it."

Kate giggled. "You know, that still sounds very weird. I'm a DI. A DI!"

"Not before time." Anderton dumped the heavy tray onto the bed with a sigh of relief. "I think my table waiting days are over."

"Bed waiting, surely."

"Those too." He waited until Kate had settled the covers back over her legs and moved the tray to her lap. "There you go. Happy—happy detective inspectoring."

"Thank you." Kate was genuinely touched. She'd been studying hard for her DI exams for several months and she and Anderton hadn't seen as much of one another as they both would have liked. Now that she'd finally achieved that elusive qualification, Kate hoped that they might rekindle the relationship that they'd been enjoying before the studying started. Not that it was *bad* now, not at all. But...well, it could be improved. She hoped Anderton felt the same way.

She tucked into her breakfast with a will. Anderton, since his forced retirement, had really developed his cooking skills. He was now a better cook than Kate had ever been.

"Oh, I forgot." Anderton picked up the last of the newspaper from the floor and assembled it in a slapdash fashion before dumping it on the bedside table. "I forgot the most important part. Hold on a sec, Kate..."

Obediently, Kate paused in her eating; it was difficult, as the smoked salmon and scrambled eggs were going down a treat. She took an anxious look at the clock as Anderton creaked off down the corridor towards the stairs. Whenever she stayed over, the drive to work took an extra twenty minutes. At least she didn't have to worry about Merlin, her cat, going hungry in the mornings anymore. She'd worked out an arrangement with her next-door neighbour, Janet. Janet would feed Merlin if Kate was away for the night, and in return, Kate would cut Janet's grass and do the other garden maintenance tasks difficult for her elderly neighbour.

Kate, her mind racing ahead, looked out of the window at the weak morning sunshine. From the bedroom window, she could see the distant green and grey of the hills that encircled Abbeyford. Although she had a key to Anderton's house, they'd never discussed whether she would eventually move in with him. Or would he move in with her? That was something else they'd not talked about. I suppose we have to, at some point, thought Kate. But it was difficult to imagine a satisfactory conversation on the subject when Kate wasn't even sure what she wanted. Did she want to move in with Anderton? She'd never lived with a partner before. Perhaps I'm too set in my ways, she thought, rather gloomily. *And if I'm not, he most definitely is.*

She was so lost in thought that she jumped as Anderton crashed the bedroom door open again.

"Ta-da—again."

Kate saw what he held in his hands – a bottle of champagne and two flute glasses. She laughed. "I can't have *that*. I've got to drive to work in a minute."

Anderton grinned. "Just a mouthful. As your senior officer, I permit it."

Kate smiled back but there was a slightly awkward pause just the same. The thing was, Anderton *wasn't* Kate's senior officer anymore. Technically, he was still a DCI, but as time went on, the idea of Anderton making a return to the Abbeyford station seemed more and more unlikely. Kate knew he'd just been making a joke, but... Shrugging, she held her hand out for the glass and Anderton sploshed a great deal more than a mouthful into it.

"Cheers," he said, clinking his glass against hers. "And I meant what I said. This promotion is not before time. You've worked really hard, Kate. I'm proud of you."

Kate blinked, her eyes suddenly stinging. Not having been showered with praise and affection for much of her life, unexpected displays of it always affected her. She sniffed, trying to smile, and thanked him. "I'm glad it's all over," she said, clearing her throat. "At least now we might be able to spend a bit more time together."

"Mmm." Anderton sounded more non-committal

than she would have liked. Almost as if he weren't listening. He tipped up his flute and emptied the dregs of the contents down his throat. Kate took a prim sip of hers and then handed him her nearly full glass.

"Here, get sozzled. I'm off to work."

"Don't tempt me." Anderton put both glasses down and moved the tray off her lap before sweeping her into his arms. "Try not to be late home tonight if you can. I've got something to talk to you about."

"I'll try." Kate felt a not-unpleasant thump in her stomach. That sounded serious. She was half tempted to ask him what it was now, but a glance at the clock told her she was really going to be late if she didn't get a wriggle on. And with the new DCI, Nicola Weaver, at the helm, late was really *not* what you wanted to be.

Anderton kissed her and released her. "Off you go then. I'm going to drink this and then—"

"Go back to sleep?" Kate grinned as she climbed out of bed.

"Probably," Anderton said with dignity.

"Have fun." Kate tipped him a wink as she made her way towards the door and the bathroom beyond.

***

IT WAS A LOVELY DRIVE to work—at least the first twenty minutes of it, as the road wound its way through countryside, past farms and fields and over the rolling expanse of the river Avon, glittering in the sunshine. It had been a fairly wet summer, and the leaves were still green, touched here and there with tints of ruby and gold. They were falling, despite their colour. Kate stopped outside the Abbeyford station doors to detach a large yellow leaf that was stubbornly adhering to the back of her shoe.

She made it to the central office with thirty seconds to spare. Under Anderton's watch, he'd never much minded if people trickled in over the course of half an hour or so, as long as you didn't take the piss and roll up at eleven o'clock. Thinking wistfully of those days, Kate hurried to her desk and switched on her computer, quickly stashing her bag and coat beneath the desk so that it looked as though she'd been there for ages.

"Well, well, well," said DS Chloe Wapping, who sat opposite her. "Late on your first day as a DI. I'm going to report this, you know. DCI Weaver needs to know." She mustered a reproachful, sober expression. "I'm surprised at you, DI Redman. I'm not just surprised, I'm *disappointed*."

Kate burst out laughing and made an eloquent, two-fingered gesture across the desk. Chloe guffawed, sober face melting away. "Alright, bird? Detective Inspector Bird?"

Kate laughed harder. "Give me a break, bird."

"Seriously, though, congratulations and all that. You've done well."

"Thanks." Kate looked up apprehensively as a

shadow fell over her desk. But instead of the dreaded figure of DCI Weaver, she caught the eye of the rather more appealing shape of DS Theo Marsh.

"All right, mate?" Kate searched his face for sarcasm but could only find his usual amiable expression. "Had a good break?"

Kate and Anderton had just been away for a three day visit to the Isle of Wight. "Not bad, thanks." She waited for the congratulations she felt sure were coming.

"Nice one. Can we have a quick word this morning when you're back in the swing of things?"

"Um—yes."

"Ta." Theo turned to amble off.

"Theo," said Chloe, in a scolding voice. "Aren't you forgetting something?"

Theo turned around in a mild panic. "Am I? What?" He caught Kate's eye and sagged with relief. "Oh, sorry, mate. Happy birthday."

Kate guffawed. "It's not my birthday, you idiot."

"It's not?" Theo clapped a hand to his stubbled jaw. "Oh my *God*. You're getting married."

Now it was Chloe's turn to laugh, whilst Kate smiled over the jolt in her stomach induced by the thought. "Theo, you idiot. She's just been made DI!"

"*Oh*." Theo heaved a gusty sigh of relief. "Yeah, I knew *that*. Just didn't—didn't want you getting a big head about it, Kate, right?"

Kate was still laughing. "So, I'm afraid this means I'm back to bossing you around, Theo."

"Ha, ha. Yeah right." For a moment, Theo's dark brows came down in a frown. Kate stopped laughing. Surely he wasn't offended by the thought? A moment later, he was smiling and she felt herself relax again. "Well, congrats and all that."

"Thanks—" Kate was interrupted by the ringing of the telephone on Chloe's desk.

"I'll get it." Chloe picked up the receiver and spoke the usual words. There was the usual moment of stillness as she listened to whatever she was being conveyed by the person on the other end of the line. Kate and Theo, veterans of these types of calls, waited tensely.

Eventually Chloe put the phone down and blew out her cheeks.

"One for us?" Kate asked, already knowing the answer.

"Yep. Elderly man's body found in his house over at Cudston Magna. Looks like a stabbing."

Kate's eyebrows went up. Stabbings were unusual when the victim was elderly. "What—" she began and then the soft voice of DCI Nicola Weaver spoke from behind her, almost in her ear. She jumped.

"Thank you, DS Redman. I'll take it from here."

Kate, recovering herself, sat back and let Chloe fill Nicola in on what they knew of the crime scene. It took her a moment to realise that Nicola had called her 'Detective Sergeant'. Given Theo had genuinely forgotten her new title, Nicola's oversight could have been an honest mistake, but then knowing Nicola, as she—unfortunately—did, Kate wondered if it were intentional.

As the two women spoke, and Theo perched himself on a nearby desk to await orders, Kate looked over at Olbeck's corner office, expecting to see him at his desk. Then she caught herself. Her friend and colleague, DI Mark Olbeck, was now on paternal leave, having recently adopted a young boy and a younger girl, siblings, with his husband Jeff. It had only been a week, but Kate missed him being there. She made a mental note to call him later to see how things were going with his brand new family. She'd promised herself that she'd leave Olbeck and Jeff to it, for the first week at least, before turning up with cards and flowers and toys and chocolate.

She brought herself back to the present as the soft but curiously penetrating voice of Nicola Weaver called them all to order. It was time to start work.

Chapter Two

IT WAS NOW KATE'S ENVIABLE position as a DI in being able to pick her subordinate for the visit to the latest crime scene. She plumped for Chloe over Theo, hoping her preference wasn't too obvious. As it happened, DCI Weaver asked to see Theo in her office just as Kate was debating how to ask for Chloe without it seeming like a rejection to Theo. She breathed an inner sigh of relief as she watched DCI Weaver waft back to her office with Theo trailing in her wake, his hands in his pockets.

"Come on, bird. Let's get going. You can fill me in on everything on the way."

"I assume I'm driving?"

Kate's smile wavered, unsure of whether Chloe was joking or not. "I don't mind," she said, a little awkwardly.

"I'll do it. I don't mind either."

They gathered up their bags and coats in a slightly artificial silence. Kate was feeling a little bit... paranoid? Was that the right word? She'd worked so hard for this qualification, this step up in seniority, but right now, she was wondering whether she'd made the right decision. The idea of her being senior to him seemed to be putting Theo's back up, and she wasn't sure how Chloe felt about it either. Not really. It was hardly the kind of thing she could ask. *Excuse me, bird, but do you mind taking orders from me, your former equal?* She remembered when Olbeck had become a DI, years back now, when she'd remained a DS. In some ways, it was fascinating seeing it from the other side, as it were. Fascinating but not very comfortable.

She made an effort to dismiss the worries from her mind and, once in the car, with the music on and *en route* to their destination, the mood lightened. Lightened as much as attending a potential murder scene would allow, thought Kate with an inner grin.

"So, who's the vic? Do we know yet?"

"Yep." Chloe was a fast but efficient driver. She didn't take her eyes from the road as she spoke. "He's been identified already—his cleaning lady found him. He's a retired teacher, some sort of academic, I think. Doctor Roland Barry."

"So, what happened?"

"It's pretty nasty, apparently. Multiple stab wounds. A lot of aggression, a lot of violence."

"Right." Kate thought for a moment. Such a crime was rare involving an elderly person. Not that it didn't happen, but... She recalled a crime scene from a previous case, where a married father of three had been found trussed and bound in leather, his head caved in like a deflated football. *Nasty*. A sad case. Shaking off the memories, Kate asked a few more questions but Chloe had reached the limit of her current knowledge of the crime.

They were out in deep countryside now, surrounded on all sides by rolling green hills, wooded here and there, with fields of gently waving wheat on either side of the road. The wind stroked the stalks as they passed, as if an invisible hand were smoothing down the furry flanks of a giant golden animal. The sky was a pale blue, heaped with whipped-cream clouds.

"What a gorgeous day," said Chloe. "Hope it keeps up for the weekend."

Kate agreed. "Mind you, after the summer we've had, we're due a bit of nice weather."

"Wasn't it sunny in the Isle of Wight—" Chloe stopped herself as she spotted the road sign for Cudston Magna. "Oh, here we are." She glanced at the sat nav. "Only a mile to go."

Roland Barry's cottage stood at the end of a long lane, the tarmac now thickly plastered with dead leaves. It was a straight road, and Kate and Chloe could see the bustle of police activity from quite a distance as they approached. Crime scene tape had already been wound about the gateposts of the garden, and the white van of the Scene of Crime Officers was pulled up on the verge. Chloe parked her car behind it and switched off the engine.

She and Kate stood for a moment when they got out of the car, surveying the scene, getting a feel for the location.

"Remote," Kate said, looking around and listening to the silence.

Chloe agreed. "Not really a place you'd stumble across, is it? Think the killer must have known where to come."

"Come on." Kate ducked under the crime scene tape, flashing her card to the uniformed officer guarding the door of the cottage. "DS Wapping and DS Redman—" She caught herself out and tried again. "*DI* Redman, from Abbeyford. Is Stephen Smithfield coordinating?"

They headed into the cottage in search of the senior crime officer, who was known to both of them through years of long service. The cottage was small and rather cosy, remarkable only in being unremarkable in its décor. Magnolia walls and beige carpeting throughout; indifferent watercolour landscapes framed on the walls. It had probably been built around the late 1800s, thought Kate, who was quite interested in architectural history. The usual layout: living room, dining room and kitchen on the ground floor. Three bedrooms upstairs, one of which would have been converted into the bathroom.

The crowd of SOCOs was thickest in the living room. Kate reached the door and braced herself. In some indefinable way, she could feel Chloe doing the same. It was as well that they did. As they entered the crowded room and saw the body, Kate sucked in her breath. They regarded the bloodstained mess on the carpet in silence.

"Nasty," said Chloe, eventually.

"Mm." There wasn't anything that Kate could really say to that. She realised that the pathologist bending over the corpse was her friend Kirsten Telling, recently back at work from her second round of maternity leave. "Kirsten, hello. How are you?"

"Hello, Kate. Chloe. I'm fine, thanks." Dr Telling looked up from what she was doing with a smile. She was an unusual looking person—a conventionally beautiful woman who looked as though she'd been stretched like rubber. Her recent pregnancy had given her a little more flesh on her bones, which suited her. "I'll be with you in a moment."

"Of course. No rush." Kate could see for herself the probable cause of death. Someone had used a knife, or perhaps several knives. The carpet beneath the body was dyed scarlet, the edges of the pool already browning as the blood dried. Its coppery tang hung thick in the air; Kate could taste it.

Grimacing, she stepped carefully over to the sideboard, where ornaments and photographs were clustered. Kate paid particular attention to the photographs, of which there were few. One was very old, sepia-toned, with the two people featured in it, poised and stiff, dressed in the clothing of seventy years ago. Roland Barry's parents, perhaps? There was a more recent photograph of the deceased himself, dressed in walking gear and posed in a landscape that Kate thought was probably the Lake District. The only other photograph was of a middle-aged woman, dressed in a fussy, flowery dress and smiling awkwardly for the camera at what looked like somebody's wedding. His wife?

"Was he married?" Kate asked Chloe.

"I don't know. I don't know anything about him, really, apart from what I've already told you." Chloe glanced about the room and threw up her hands. "God, where are we even going to start? There's no neighbours, no CCTV..."

"Well, let's talk to his cleaner first, if she's recovered from the shock."

Chloe concurred. "She's in the kitchen, I think."

Making their way through the house, they ran into the senior investigator, Stephen Smithfield, who greeted them in his usual, absent-minded fashion; it was as if they'd come across one another at a dinner party, rather than a brutal crime scene. Stephen was well known for never, ever being fazed by any of the horrible deaths he encountered. It made him rather unnerving company, but it did at least mean he was very good at his job.

"Morning, ladies." Stephen blinked at them amiably through his glasses. "See the body yet?"

"Yes, we have." Kate thought back to the shocking sight in the living room. "Pretty brutal."

"Indeed," Stephen said cheerfully. "Judging from the blood loss, I imagine he died pretty quickly, though. Multiple stab wounds, immense blood loss. Unusual, isn't it? In this kind of setting, I mean. Anyway, I must get on. Talk to you in a bit."

Kate and Chloe exchanged glances and grins as Stephen bustled off down the corridor. "Come on, let's see if we can find the cleaner," murmured Kate, conscious of the fact that the kitchen door stood ajar.

Roland Barry's cleaner was a large, middle-aged lady exhibiting the usual behaviour of a person unfortunate enough to find a body. She was pale and trembling and plaiting her chubby fingers together. A uniformed officer, one of the victim support officers, sat next to her and had draped a blanket around her shoulders. Kate recognised her face but couldn't put a name to the officer. Victim support tended to be female. Kate suspected there was something inherently sexist about that, but this was not the time for a lengthy analysis of exactly why she felt that.

The officer looked up as Kate and Chloe approached. "Good morning. This is Sandra Cuckfield. She cleans for Mr Barry."

"Hello, Mrs Cuckfield," said Kate, as gently as she could. "Now I realise you've had a terrible shock, but I was wondering if you feel up to answering a few questions? You can take as much time as you need."

Mrs Cuckfield gulped and held a disintegrating tissue up to her watering eyes. "Yes – I will, if I can."

"Let me get you another tissue," Chloe said, looking about the kitchen for a box. The uniformed officer pushed one towards her. "I'm DS Wapping and this is DI Redman." Both Kate and she showed their identification. Mrs Cuckfield blinked at them in silence whilst they sat down.

"Now, could you just run through what happened this morning, Mrs Cuckfield?" asked Kate, unobtrusively taking out her notebook and pen. She was aware of Chloe doing the same.

Mrs Cuckfield gulped again. "I come weekly, every Tuesday. There's never very much that needs to be done; it's mostly just dusting and hoovering." She wiped her eyes with the fresh tissue and took a deep breath. "I get here about ten o'clock—"

"Do you have a key?" Chloe asked. Mrs Cuckfield nodded.

"Would Doctor Barry normally be here when you come?" asked Kate.

"Not always. Sometimes he was, and sometimes he wasn't. I always ring the bell before I come in, just to give him warning, like, that I'm about to come in. He was a very private man."

Kate's ears pricked up. "Would you say you knew him well, Mrs Cuckfield?"

She was disappointed a moment later when the woman shook her head. "No, I wouldn't say that. I've cleaned for him for about two years but I didn't really know him. He was friendly enough, like, but we didn't really ever *chat* or anything."

"Doctor Barry lived alone, then?"

"Yes, he wasn't married. I think he has a sister, yes, he does—did." She stumbled over the correct tense. "He *did* have a sister; he used to mention that he'd had lunch with her occasionally."

"Any children?" asked Kate.

Sandra Cuckfield shook her head once more. "No, not that I know of. He was a proper bachelor."

Kate nodded, thinking. Had Roland Barry been homosexual? And if so, did that have any bearing on the manner of his death? Had he picked someone up or had a date with a killer?

Total speculation, Kate. She listened as Sandra Cuckfield falteringly described her meagre relationship to the deceased. They would have to try and get hold of the sister she'd mentioned. The dead man seemed to have led a lonely life. Perhaps the secret to his death was somewhere here in this remote cottage. She began to feel impatient, wanting to get on with the search into cupboards and filing cabinets, but she forced the feeling down and stoically made notes as Mrs Cuckfield continued to talk.

Chapter Three

AN HOUR LATER, MRS CUCKFIELD had been carted off to Abbeyford Police Station to make an official statement. The body of the unfortunate Roland Barry had been removed and the scene of crime officers were busy measuring, collating and collecting forensic evidence and data. Kate and Chloe, released from their interview with the first witness, were able to begin the slow search of Roland Barry's belongings in an effort to find out more about him.

The house was sparsely furnished, his bedroom almost austere. There were no more photographs in the house and only a few pictures dotted here and there. Two pictures showed the same lake, set against a mountain range. Kate unhooked one that hung in the hallway upstairs and carried it into the bedroom to compare it.

"That's the same place, isn't it?" she asked Chloe, inclining the other picture frame to show her friend.

"Looks like it. Looks like the Lake District to me." Chloe glanced at Kate, her eyebrows raised. "Think it's significant?"

"It could be. It might be a place he once lived or liked to holiday in. Not many people have more than one original watercolour of the same place unless it's of some significance to them." Kate gently propped the picture up against the wall. "Anyway, unless I'm much mistaken, that filing cabinet in the spare bedroom will tell us a lot of what we need to know."

They headed to the spare room, and Kate pulled the top drawer of the cabinet open. "Luckily it's not locked."

The contents were neatly filed. Doctor Barry had seemingly been a methodical man. Kate knelt before the grey metal cabinet and flicked through the contents, noting the labels on the folders. *Car, Insurance, Certificates*. From this last, she withdrew a yellowing piece of paper—Roland Barry's birth certificate. He'd been born in 1954, in Watford, London, putting him well into his sixties on the date of his death. Kate brought the entire folder out and opened it up on the dusty floorboards. There were certificates proving his qualification as a teacher, and then as a PhD. So, an academic doctor, not a medical one.

Chloe's gloved hands were methodically going through the drawers of the only other significant piece of furniture in the room other than the single bed.

"Anything?" asked Kate.

Chloe shook her head in disappointment. "Nothing

much. Junk, mostly." She shut the final bottom drawer with a slam and got up from her knees. "We should really do the main bedroom first, hey?"

"You do that." Kate wanted to sort through the paperwork more thoroughly. She looked up as a thought struck her. "We'll have to get the sister to come in, do an official identification. She sounds as though she might be the only person able to give us a rundown of the victim."

"I'll ring Rav and get him to track her down. Also to just do a general search on Barry." Chloe pulled her mobile from her handbag as she was speaking. She glanced around the sad little sparsely furnished room. "Maybe he's not the harmless old duffer that he appears."

"Are they ever?" Kate didn't wait for an answer to her rhetorical question. She gathered up a bundle of cardboard folders in her arms and went to find a more comfortable seating position on the bed.

**

IT WAS A LONG DAY, as first days on new cases tended to be. After hours spent at Roland Barry's cottage, and an equally lengthy time back in the office, it was nearly ten o'clock by the time Kate called it a night. She'd been due over at Anderton's that evening but, exhausted, she rang him as she was leaving the office.

"Hey, you."

"Hullo. You sound knackered."

"I am. That's what I was calling about."

Kate could hear the smile of recognition in Anderton's voice. "I take it that you're heading straight back to your place instead?"

"Yes. Sorry. You know what it's like." Kate caught herself and cursed inwardly. She tried very hard not to keep reminding Anderton of what he had lost, but sometimes it just slipped out. "Um, I mean—"

"Don't worry." Anderton sounded wry rather than annoyed. "Anyway, I've got some hardcore Game of Thrones to catch up on, so you've given me the opportunity to do just that."

"Happy to oblige." Kate, safe in the knowledge that he couldn't see her, pulled a face. Sometimes she felt like the only person left in England who didn't like that bloody TV series. She remembered that Anderton had said that morning that he wanted to talk to her about something. Briefly, she considered bringing it up and just as quickly decided not to. If it was important enough, it should be a face-to-face conversation. Plus, she was knackered.

They said goodbye and she slung her phone back in her handbag. Trotting down the steps, she saw Theo's tall figure leaning against the handrails and pulling hard on his e-cigarette. A cloud of vapour escaped from his mouth into the cold night air.

"Theo," said Kate, somewhat surprised. He had the unmistakeable aura of someone waiting for someone else. "Bit late for one of your hot dates, hey?"

Theo grinned. "Never too late for one of those, mate. Actually, I'm just waiting on a taxi."

"I can run you home if you want?"

Theo shook his head. "Nah, thanks all the same. It'll be here any minute."

"OK. See you tomorrow, then."

Theo blew her a smoke ring—or should that be vape ring?—in farewell, and Kate headed off to her car. It was very cold by now, and she'd come out that morning without a decent coat. Shivering, she turned the car heater up to full and drove off.

Her route home took her past the front of the police station, and she was surprised to see Theo—or someone who looked very like him—striding off down the road accompanied by another person. It was too dark to see who it was. Hadn't he said he was waiting for a taxi? Kate pondered for a moment and then forgot about it, concentrating on her drive home.

***

THE FIRST DEBRIEF OF THE Barry case took place the following morning. The whole team (minus Olbeck) were assembled in the incident room, waiting for DCI Weaver to grace them with her presence.

Kate sat next to Chloe, chatting about nothing in particular. She spotted Theo across the room, yawning hugely. It was contagious. Kate stifled her own yawn, unfortunately just as Nicola Weaver came into the room and caught her.

"I do hope we're not keeping you up, DI Redman."

Nicola's genius—and Kate had to admit it, begrudgingly—was to fire off the kind of bitchy remark that, taken one way, could merely be gentle teasing banter, and in the other way, a nasty, mean-spirited dig. Kate knew damn well the way that Nicola had meant it. She'd worked out a way of dealing with it, for it happened a lot; pretending that DCI Weaver had meant it lightheartedly and responding as if she had.

"No, I'm fine," Kate said, with a light laugh, keeping the smile on her face. She felt Chloe snort quietly beside her and the smile became genuine. She and Chloe were good mates anyway, but they were further bonded by their hatred and loathing of their boss.

"Good," Nicola said with a wintry smile. "We're debriefing on the Roland Barry murder case, as you all no doubt know." She cast a glance about the room. "The body has been formally identified by his sister, Mrs Winifred Cole."

Kate made a mental note of the name. That would be someone to interview as soon as humanly possible.

Nicola was still speaking. "The post mortem is scheduled for first thing tomorrow morning. Theo, would you be our representative, please?"

"Yup." Theo nodded. Nicola favoured him with a slightly warmer smile before turning away.

Oh, so he's 'Theo' but I'm DI Redman. Kate's mood

soured. It was made worse by the sheer pettiness of the behaviour—or that Kate would seem even more petty if she complained about it.

"DS Wapping, DS Cheetam, could you begin to sift through all the CCTV, the witness statements—make a head start on what will no doubt be a long job?"

"Right you are," Chloe said, in a tone just the right side of sarcastic. Nicola favoured her with a cold look, indicating she wasn't fooled. Then she turned away, dismissing them.

"I'll be in my office if anyone needs me. Please make an appointment through Pauline first."

They all held their collective breath as Nicola shut the office door quietly behind her. Then, almost to a man, they exhaled.

"She's such a cow," sighed Chloe, beginning to walk back to her desk.

"You'll have no argument from me on that." Kate followed her friend. "But, given that that's a given, what are we going to do about it?"

"Well, I for one intend to moan loudly and pointlessly for some time," Chloe said, grinning and flinging herself down in her chair.

"Good plan." Kate brought her computer screen to life and groaned aloud at the long list of unread emails. *Coffee, I need coffee.* She got up to make them all one and then sat down, mentally squaring her shoulders at the amount of work she had to do.

Chapter Four

WINIFRED COLE, THE LATE ROLAND Barry's sister, lived in the small village of Starford, some ten miles outside of Abbeyford. Kate was driving and had detoured to pick Chloe up from her little fisherman's cottage in Salterton.

"God, I love this time of year," Kate said as they sped along the bypass. "Autumn is my favourite season."

Chloe gave her an incredulous look. "You're joking, right? It's getting colder, it's damp, winter's coming..."

"Yes but—new boots. Log fires. Blackberries. Halloween!"

"Oh, God, you don't celebrate that, do you?"

"I *love* Halloween. I might even have a little party this year." Kate gave her friend a mischievous glance. "Dressing up and everything. You'll come, right?"

Chloe rolled her eyes. "If I have to. Will there be any unattached males invited?"

"Erm—" Kate did a quick mental tally as to all the unattached males she knew who might be able to cope with Chloe. It was a fairly short list. "Um...a few."

"Well, I might consider it." Chloe looked gloomily out of the window. "It's been ages since I've had a date. Let alone a shag."

Kate laughed. "What about Theo?"

Chloe and Theo had dated very briefly on her arrival at Abbeyford. Kate wasn't particularly surprised it hadn't gone anywhere. Both Chloe and Theo were a bit too alpha to really be compatible.

Chloe rolled her eyes. "I've learnt my lesson about dipping my pen in the office ink, as it were." She gave Kate a mischievous look of her own. "I know it worked out for *you,* but we can't all be that lucky." She reached for the heater control on the dashboard and turned it up a little. "Besides, I think Theo might have someone else on the go."

Kate snorted. "*Someone* else? How about several someone elses?"

"I don't know," said Chloe. "I think he's had enough of playing the field. When we had our brief—erm, *liaison*, I got the impression he wanted to settle down a bit. Have a proper relationship. Unfortunately, that wasn't going to be with me."

Kate raised her eyebrows, considering. She was so used to thinking of Theo as the classic playboy—a girl in every port, despite the fact that he wasn't a sailor—that it was difficult to think that he might want something more meaningful. "I suppose you could be right," she said, thinking aloud. "I mean, things have changed a bit, haven't they? Rav's married, Mark's married—and now with children. Me and Anderton are together. Poor Theo hasn't got anyone to play with anymore, has he?" She grinned at Chloe. "Except you."

"Ha! Not likely. I wish him well though, the cocky little bugger." Chloe glanced at the sat nav. "We're almost there, anyway."

***

WINIFRED COLE'S HOUSE WAS A non-descript semi-detached, built in the 1960s, with a red-tiled roof and small, neat front garden. The street was narrow, and Kate had to wait impatiently several times for cars to give way for her to carry on to where the house was located. Eventually, she found a parking space several doors down and swung the car in to the curb.

Winifred Cole was a small, spare woman, rather anxious in demeanour, and with carefully curled white hair. She was hesitant to talk at first, but once the officers had been supplied with tea and biscuits, and installed on the mushroom-coloured sofa, she seemed to relax a little.

Kate gave her the standard words of condolence, hoping that she at least sounded sincere. She *was* sincere, actually; no matter how long you'd been in the job, it was never nice to see people floored by grief. Not that this exactly appeared the case here. Mrs Cole didn't seem particularly happy but she didn't seem particularly upset, either. Kate decided to find out why.

"Were you close to your brother, Mrs Cole?" she asked.

Mrs Cole sniffed. "Not particularly, I don't think. I mean, he was *family*." She didn't elaborate on that. Instead she asked whether they would like another biscuit.

"Not just now, thanks, Mrs Cole," said Kate, not wanting her witness to disappear off into the kitchen again. "So, you wouldn't say you were close? Would he confide in you, would you say?"

"Well—" Mrs Cole seemed at a loss. "Well, perhaps, if it were something really worrying him."

"Did he seemed worried about anything when you last saw him?" That would have been on the day of his death, but Kate didn't want to remind Mrs Cole of that, in case it interfered with her memories.

"No, dear. No, I don't think so. We had lunch, you know, where we always do—in the café in John Lewis."

"What did you talk about, Mrs Cole?" asked Chloe. Kate noticed she had a biscuit crumb stuck to her lower lip, but she couldn't exactly tell her in front of a witness.

Mrs Cole looked unhappy, or if not exactly unhappy then a bit lost. "Well, I can't really remember, dear. Um...Roland was planning a holiday, I remember that much. We talked a bit about that."

"Where was he going to go?" As Chloe spoke, Kate saw the biscuit crumb fall from her lip, to her relief.

"He liked Asia. He'd been to a lot of places in East

Asia. Vietnam and Thailand and, um, what's the other one he mentioned? Laos. That was where he was planning to go this year."

"So, he was well travelled, then, Mrs Cole?" Kate decided she'd better speak up for a change.

"Yes, Roland loved to travel. He couldn't afford to go more than once a year or so, especially now he was on his pension, but he did enjoy it."

Kate remembered the picture of the Lake District. "Who would he travel with? He wasn't married, was he?"

Mrs Cole shook her head. "No, he never got married. He had girlfriends, of course—he wasn't a homosexual, if that's what you're thinking." Kate and Chloe managed not to exchange glances. "He was engaged to someone once, Lucinda Somebody. Oh, what was her surname? I can't remember, off hand. But that didn't last, and the wedding never took place." Mrs Cole clasped her hands together and for once, became eloquent. "I really don't know who could have done this awful thing to Roland, I truly don't." Behind her glasses, her eyes were bewildered and shone with unshed tears. "It must be some madman, some serial killer. It can't be anyone who knew him. Everyone liked him. He... I—I just can't understand it."

"I'm really so very sorry," Chloe said in her warmest, most sympathetic tone, and DS Wapping could be extremely warm and sympathetic when she wanted to be. Mrs Cole wiped her eyes with a crumpled tissue, sniffing.

They carried on the interview after a discreet

pause, asking gently about Roland's finances, his friends, his last place of work, his neighbours. Nothing was particularly illuminating. Roland Barry's nearest neighbour was half a mile down the lane, his friends mostly ex-colleagues who lived in places all over the UK. Kate scribbled down the names that she could interview, but it was a sparse list. Barry had apparently last worked five years before, at a sixth-form college in Bath, but since his retirement, he had occasionally privately tutored children and teenagers. Kate remembered seeing some folders in the filing cabinet at Barry's house and made a mental note to go through each and every bit of paperwork contained within that cabinet with a fine-tooth comb.

***

LATER THAT AFTERNOON, DRIVING HOME, Kate made the impulsive decision to go and call on Olbeck. It seemed like longer than a week since she had seen him; she'd purposely stayed away, wanting to give him and Jeff the space and time they needed with their new young children. But now, driving through the part of town in which he lived, she felt a pull towards her friend's house. She debated sending him a text and then decided against it. On a second thought, she pulled into a petrol station and bought wine and flowers (for Olbeck and Jeff) and chocolate lollipops for the children. Was that bad? Perhaps she should have bought something healthier—satsumas, or bananas or something...

Fretting a little, she drove on towards Olbeck's house. He probably won't even be in, thought Kate. How old were the children again? She knew they were a sibling pair; a boy and a girl. Feeling more nervous than the situation perhaps warranted, Kate parked the car in the driveway and made her way to the front door, clutching her gifts to her chest in the absence of a plastic bag.

She was half expecting to hear childish shrieks and thuds and see toys flying out of the window and other markers of domestic chaos. Ridiculous, really, because when Olbeck opened the door, all was calm within.

"Kate!" He swept her into a hug and the lollipops fell to the floor. The flowers got crushed. Luckily, Kate retained a firm grip on the wine bottle. "Oh, sorry."

"Thought I'd pop in, see if you're surviving," said Kate. She and Olbeck retrieved the sweets. "I bought these for—for the children. Do say if they're not allowed to have chocolate yet."

Olbeck grinned. "Well, Poppy's only eight months so probably best not—"

Kate was crestfallen. "Sorry."

"Don't be daft. *I'll* eat it. Harry can have one."

They moved back through to the rear of the house where the kitchen and dining room had been thrown together into one big, sunny space. Jeff, who was a keen cook, had overseen the installation of a very swish kitchen, and the remaining space had become a calm, bright, relaxing room, with minimal ornaments, a large corner sofa in a dusky blue shade and a fluffy white rug.

Now, the room looked as if a toyshop and a baby equipment factory had exploded within it. The clean lines of the wide wooden floorboards were lost beneath a sea of toys, baby bouncers, rattles, dummies, packs of nappies, stray white muslin cloths, a half-sucked rice cake, crayons, teddy bears and baby wipe packets. The hitherto hospital-quality cleanliness and sterility of the kitchen was but a distant dream, wiped away by half-empty baby bottles, jars of baby food and a large round object puffing steam that Kate couldn't quite work out the function of, before a long-ago memory told her it was a bottle steriliser.

Jeff, looking harassed but happy, sat in the middle of the chaos with a baby on his lap; curls of fair hair covering her round head, one cheek bright pink. She was wailing loudly. Over in the corner sat a boy of about two or three, thin and wary looking, with rather long brown hair. He had his knees tight to his chest and had his thumb in his mouth.

"Kate," said Jeff, or rather shouted it above the noise. "What a lovely surprise! Come and meet the kids!"

"Hello," Kate said to the wailing baby, or rather mouthed it as she couldn't hear herself think.

"Sorry about this, Poppy's teething," shouted Jeff.

"I'll just pop upstairs and see if I can find some gel for her gums."

"Okay," mouthed Kate, smiling desperately.

Poppy's wails floated behind her as Jeff took her out of the room. Kate tried not to relax too obviously.

She smiled at the little boy—Harry, wasn't it? "Hello, Harry. I'm Kate."

Harry looked at her unblinkingly.

"He gets a bit anxious when Poppy cries," said Olbeck. "Or when there's a lot of noise." He addressed the boy. "It's okay, Harry. Nothing to worry about. Do you want me to get you Tato?" Harry nodded in a movement so tiny Kate could barely see it. "Okay, sweetheart. You just wait there and Kate and I will go and find him."

In the hallway, Olbeck gave Kate a smile that she could tell was meant to reassure. "Sorry about that, it's just he gets frightened if I leave him with strangers. Not that you're a stranger but, you know—"

"I am to him," said Kate. She squeezed her friend's arm. "I get it, it's okay. I'm sorry—I should have given you warning I was coming around—"

"Don't be silly. It's lovely to see you." Olbeck had gone into the front living room and was hunting around. "I have to find Tato. He's Harry's favourite cuddly toy."

"What's he look like?" Kate asked, joining him in the search.

"Like a big potato, of course."

"A cuddly *potato*? Interesting." Kate spied some-thing likely wedged down between the sofa and the armchair. "Is this the fellow?"

"Oh, well done. Here, you come and give it to Harry. And the lollipop. If all else fails, try bribery."

They went back into the back room, where Harry hadn't moved a muscle. "Here you go, sweetheart," said Olbeck, ushering Kate forward with the precious Tato. "Here he is."

There was so much love in his voice that Kate found herself blinking back unexpected tears. Smiling, she held Tato out to Harry and waited patiently for him to take his toy.

Chapter Five

IT WAS CHLOE WHO TOOK the call a few days later. She, Kate, Rav and Theo were all in the office, beginning the laborious task of wading through the mountains of paperwork, evidence and forensic reports that littered their desks.

The telephone ringing in the background was just another noise at first. It wasn't until Chloe picked up the receiver and answered, rather absently, before tensing and asking the caller to repeat themselves, that the others picked up on the fact that another serious crime had been discovered.

Kate, Rav and Theo listened to Chloe's terse responses, watching her rapidly scribble down the salient facts. Kate tried to read what was being written upside down but it was hopeless. Chloe's handwriting was bad enough at the best of times, let alone when viewed from the wrong angle.

Eventually, Chloe replaced the receiver and looked up to a row of expectant faces.

"Well?" demanded Theo.

Chloe rolled her eyes. "Well, what do you think?"

"Murder," Rav said succinctly.

"Got it in one. Young woman, over in Arbuthon Green, found this morning by her boyfriend."

"How nice," said Kate. "Do they have a cause of death yet?"

"Looks like strangulation, apparently." Chloe pushed her chair away the desk. "I'll just go and run it past *mein Führer* and see who she wants on it."

Kate found herself hoping quite strongly that, for once, Nicola might throw a bone her way. She was finding herself frustrated with the Roland Barry case. They didn't seem to be getting anywhere; not in motive, not in suspects, and not even in establishing any of the dead man's relationships. Kate, from the benefit of years of experience, suspected that the Barry case might be one of those unsatisfying jobs which were never concluded. Not every case was solved; she knew that to her cost. Perhaps this new case might be more...*rewarding* was perhaps the wrong word to use about a situation that had violently cost someone her life, but that was how Kate felt. She walked back to her desk, superstitiously crossing her fingers that Chloe would come back from Nicola Weaver's office with good news.

***

SHE DIDN'T HAVE TO WAIT long. Chloe returned after five minutes looking neutral.

"Well?" asked Kate, trying not to sound too eager.

"She wants you to go. She wants me and Theo to debrief her on where we're at with the Barry case." Chloe rolled her eyes. "No doubt just an excuse to bitch about how we're not getting anywhere."

"Well, it makes no sense that she's sending me away then," joked Kate.

Chloe grinned reluctantly. "It's probably part of some nefarious plot we haven't worked out yet."

Kate squeezed her arm. "Good luck, bird. I'll take Rav with me, if he's free."

"Details are on my desk." Chloe gave her a half-hearted wave as she trailed back to her desk.

As it transpired, Rav was tied up with an interview, so Kate left him a note and sent him an email as back-up, asking him to join her at the scene when he was able. She drove away from the station feeling light-hearted. Even the thought she was going to view another murder scene couldn't dampen her spirits. It was another lovely autumn day; the air was sharp and crisp, and golden sunlight illuminated the vivid colour of the leaves like a slowly burning bonfire.

She'd just reached the fringes of Arbuthon Green when her mobile phone rang. It was Anderton. She pulled into a bus stop and answered it.

"Hey, you," was his opening line.

"Hello. I can't talk for long, I'm just on my way to a case—"

Although she'd tried to sound breezy and matter-of-fact, she couldn't help the fact that Anderton sounded a little bit...huffy. "Oh, fine, fine. I'm sure you've got lots of important things to do."

"Don't be like that," Kate said awkwardly. "What's the problem?"

"There's no *problem*. I just thought it might be nice if we, you know, spent some time together? For a change?"

Kate bit back what she wanted to say, which was that Anderton should know damn well how all-encompassing a murder case could be. Two murder cases, as it appeared they now had. Not that he would know that. Even as she thought, Kate felt the first qualm. Abbeyford had had its tragedies and its crimes, that was for sure, but murder itself was fairly unusual. *Two* murder cases, almost in as many days? Bad luck or something else?

"Kate?" She realised she'd gone silent for so long that Anderton was starting to sound a little worried.

"I'm here. Sorry."

"Oh, look, I can tell you're up to your eyes in it. Just give me a ring later, if you get a moment."

"Okay," Kate said absently, still thinking about the case. She heard Anderton snort as he hung up and felt a momentary surge of guilt. She was on the verge of ringing him back when the blast of a bus horn came from behind her, and she jumped and mouthed a guilty 'sorry' at the scowling face of the bus driver.

***

ARBUTHON GREEN HAD BEEN ONE of the poorer areas of the affluent town. The second murder of Kate's career in Abbeyford had been discovered there. Years later, it was slowly gentrifying; the rubbish and the graffiti had mostly disappeared, and although the houses were still shabby and run down, here and there you could see that they had been bought by people who cared about outward appearances. Some had been renovated entirely. They looked smart enough but somehow uneasy, as if the houses themselves were aware of how unconvincing the veneer of respectability actually was.

The address Kate was seeking was in a 1960s block of flats set back from the main road and with a car park at the back of the building. Discarded plastic bags and empty crisp packets swirled about Kate's legs as she locked the car. The windows of the building had a blind look, obscured as they were by blinds and grubby net curtains.

The scene of crime officers had obviously been there for some time, and the small flat on the third floor of the building felt crammed with white-suited people. Kate ducked under the crime scene tape at the door after showing her credentials. The uniform on the door had directed her to the living room in a very respectful tone. "It's the first on the left down the corridor, Detective Inspector." Unreasonable as it might be, Kate still got a small thrill from hearing her new title. The flat was warm and stuffy; too many bodies—living ones—and not enough air.

Kate found the doorway of the living room, where the body was located. She braced herself as she took her first look, but it was nothing as bad as the abattoir someone had made of Roland Barry's front room. *It's different*, she thought, feeling the knot of tension she'd been carrying around loosen in the pit of her stomach.

The body of the young woman lay on the floor, feet towards the door, head towards the one window of the room. She was dressed in a pair of black, stretchy yoga-pants, a loose pink sweatshirt on her upper half. Blonde hair covered her face, stiffened here and there with dried blood. She was slim and muscular, her feet bare, toenails painted in chipped pink varnish. The doctor bending over the body was Ivor Gatkiss, one of the regular team from the pathology labs. He greeted Kate in his usual pleasant, shy manner.

"Anything yet, Ivor?" Kate knew she was pushing her luck but it was always worth asking.

"Not much, yet, Kate. Give me half an hour or so and I'll see what I can do."

"Rightio." Kate knelt down carefully near the body, looking at it closely. The woman wasn't as young as Kate had first placed her, misled by the slimness and fitness. Close up, Kate could see the lines on her face, half-hidden under messy hair. Forties, perhaps, rather than the twenty-something that Kate had first thought.

The boyfriend had discovered the body and would

have to be interviewed, perhaps under caution. Was he still there? Kate knew as well as any officer that the most likely suspect in a murder case such as this—in the victim's own home, no sign of a break-in or intruder—were the closest relatives and loved ones of the deceased. Depressing, but there you go... Kate clambered back to her feet, suppressing a middle-aged groan, and moved towards the window, trying not to get in the way of all the white-suited forensic experts.

The room itself was decorated in a rather uninspiring fashion. It was comfortable enough, but shabby, messy and cluttered. Kate had the impression that the woman—what was her name? She hadn't even found that out yet—hadn't been particularly well off. The furniture was cheap flat-pack stuff, or obvious hand-me-downs from richer acquaintances. There was a small bookcase in the corner, and Kate went to examine the titles. You could sometimes tell a lot about a person by their taste in books. Mind you, she'd once caught Chloe reading a *Mills and Boon* romance on her lunch break, so what did that say?

Kate smiled at the memory, and of Chloe's rather too emphatic protests that she'd just found it 'lying around', and knelt on the floor by the bookcase. There was a small, rather uninspiring collection of fiction. The majority of the titles were non-fiction, with a distinctly New Age bent. Books on essential oils, aromatherapy, life-coaching, yoga. Several well-known self-help books. Kate couldn't very well start a full-scale search of the flat just yet, but it was useful just to get a feel for the kind of person the deceased woman had been.

There were few photographs on display. One of a family group, taken some time back in the eighties, if the clothes were anything to go by. Kate presumed that the teenage girl in the photograph, surrounded by what looked like her parents and slightly older brother, was the woman in the flat. What *was* her name? Kate looked around and saw, with pleasure, that Rav was coming into the room, looking rather wet, his black hair dewed all over.

He didn't greet her immediately, concentrating, like the good officer that he was, on the body. Kate walked over. "Raining out, is it, Rav?"

"Cats and dogs," he said absently, staring at Doctor Gatkiss and the body. "Anything yet?"

"Not yet. Here, come out of the way." Kate drew him back towards the corridor. "I was going to see if the boyfriend's still here. This sounds ridiculous, but I don't even have the name of the vic yet."

"Here, I can help." Rav withdrew his notebook from his pocket with a flourish. "She's Amanda Jane Callihan. Forty-three years old, lives alone, works as a yoga teacher."

That explained the woman's toned physique, thought Kate. She left Rav to observe Doctor Gatkiss's patient ministrations and made her way to the kitchen. It took about five seconds to find it; the flat was not large.

The boyfriend was still there and was being comforted by one of the uniformed officers. 'Boyfriend' was a bit of a mis-nomer; this man was clearly in his late forties or early fifties, balding at the temples with something of a paunch which strained against his sweatshirt. For all that, he was not unattractive. He wore that stunned look that Kate was fairly familiar with in this situation. It was very hard to fake that level of shock and surprise, and she made a mental note in his favour that he may not have had anything to do with his girlfriend's death.

"This is Dermot McGuigan," said the officer standing beside him. Dermot sat on the only chair in the tiny galley kitchen, a tall stool that looked too spindly to bear his weight. He wasn't crying—yet—but Kate had a feeling tears were only a few moments away. She introduced herself, showed her credentials, and added the usual words of condolence. Dermot didn't look as though he'd heard any of it.

"Mr McGuigan? Are you all right to talk with me for a minute?"

She could see him making a huge effort to pull himself together. "Yes. Sorry. Yes, I will."

"I understand you were Ms Callihan's partner? How long have you been together?"

Dermot brushed his eyes. "Um, not long. Maybe six months or so."

"Can you tell me a bit about Amanda? We'd really like to get a sort of picture of her as a person. I understand she was a yoga teacher?"

"Yeah. She did a bit of aromatherapy as well, but it was mostly yoga. I dunno... It's not really my scene, but she was really into it, all that kind of alternative stuff..." He trailed off, staring into space.

"Did she have any family?"

"No. No, she didn't have any kids."

"Sorry, Mr McGuigan, I mean, did she have parents? Siblings?"

Dermot rubbed his eyes again. He looked suddenly not so much grief-stricken, as tired. "Oh, right. Sorry. Her mum and dad were dead. She had a sister, I think, but she don't live here, in England I mean. I think she's in Scotland. Not sure."

Kate scribbled a note. That would have to be looked into. "Did she seem worried about anything, Mr McGuigan? Did she ever mention anyone who'd been threatening her?"

At this last question, Dermot McGuigan gave a dry sob, putting one hand up to his mouth. Kate waited patiently. After a long moment, he shook his head. "No. There was nothing. Nobody. She never told me nothing like that."

Kate was beginning to think that this was a waste of her time. She'd be better off tracking down Amanda Callihan's sister.

She gently drew the interview with Dermot

McGuigan to a close and left him in the capable hands of the victim liaison officer. They would arrange for his statement back at Abbeyford Station. Kate walked back through to the living room, where Rav was waiting for Doctor Gatkiss to finish his work.

As Kate stepped through the doorway, she felt a jump of—of *something*. Unease? Suspicion? Something had snagged her intuition. Not in a big way, more the gentle poke of a finger. She stopped dead and stood for a moment, staring ahead. What had it been?

"What's up?" asked Rav, who'd seen her abrupt halt.

"Not sure." Kate put her hands on her hips and swivelled her gaze about the room. Nothing jumped out at her. "There was something as I walked in... Something..."

She trailed off, not sure what she was saying. Rav kept silent. Kate looked at the room again, looked at the body and blew out her cheeks, frustrated. Whatever subconscious flag had been raised was gone.

"No good?"

"No." Kate huffed a sigh, knowing how her mind worked. Whatever she'd noticed or realised might come back, but when? And what if it didn't?

"Don't worry about it," soothed Rav.

"I won't." Kate put the matter to the back of her mind and joined him, both of them waiting for Doctor Gatkiss to finish and tell them anything he'd found out.

Chapter Six

LATE AS SHE HAD BEEN in leaving work that evening, Kate texted her neighbour to ask her to feed Merlin and headed straight for Anderton's cottage. She had a feeling she would be pushing her luck to head home again without seeing her partner. That thought made her smile a little because, to Kate, Olbeck had always been her 'partner'—well, until he got promoted. Kate added another item to her mental to-do list (which never seemed to grow any shorter): *ring Mark and Jeff.* That would have to wait until tomorrow, though.

The roads to Anderton's rural cottage were very narrow. Kate, used to them by now, hummed to herself as she drove along. Another thought jumped, unbidden, into her head. Could she see herself living here? Did she want to be quite so cut off from the town? Whilst the village in which Anderton lived was picture-postcard pretty, its only amenities were a pub and a tiny convenience store that doubled as the post office. Decent restaurants, cinemas, bars and leisure centres were miles away in Abbeyford.

Should she and Anderton even move in together

at all? *He hasn't asked you yet, Kate.* But should she be waiting for an invitation? She was a modern woman; it wasn't beyond her to ask him. Pondering the thought, she wondered whether he would consider moving in with her and Merlin. That was the trouble with partnering up rather later in life, thought Kate. One of you, if you were lucky enough to own your own house, would be giving up something you'd probably spent years working to achieve.

And besides all this, did she actually *want* to live with Anderton? She liked her house, her own space, her routines. She'd spent a lot of time and effort on making her home a comfortable and attractive place to live and it would be a wrench—much more than a wrench—to have to leave it. And didn't someone say domesticity was the death of romance? Kate puffed out her breath in a sigh as she swung into the driveway of Anderton's house. All this musing would have to wait. She was probably jumping ahead of herself by miles, anyway.

Shaking off her recent thoughts, Kate locked the car and made her way to the door. Before she could fit her key into the lock, it was opened for her.

"About time," Anderton said. It was still a slight shock to see him dressed in something that wasn't a suit.

"Nice to see you too," Kate said, grinning and holding her face up for a kiss. "I've been flat out all day."

"And now you're going to be flat out all night."

With those words, Anderton swept her up in his arms. Kate shrieked.

Laughing, Anderton heaved her over to the stairs, put one foot on the bottom tread and clearly thought better of it. "How about the sofa, instead?"

Kate was laughing too hard to answer. This was the Anderton of old, returned; ebullient, lustful and strong. Even so, he was puffing quite hard by the time he deposited her—dumped, may have been a better word—on the leather sofa. Kate's breath was becoming shorter already.

After all the amusement of the past few minutes, the tempo changed abruptly. Anderton kissed her slowly, taking his time, holding her face with tenderness in the way he knew she loved. They undressed minimally, taking off only what was necessary, keeping their hands on one another as if to keep the connection between them unbroken.

Afterwards, they lay in a damp and happy tangle on the floor, Kate's head on Anderton's broad chest. She listened to the slowing beat of his heart, the push of his chest against her cheekbone gradually decreasing in rhythm.

"God, this floor's uncomfortable," Anderton said after a few minutes. "I think I might be getting a bit old for sex that isn't conducted horizontally."

Kate lifted her head. "You're only as old as the woman you feel, they say."

"Well, exactly." Kate gave a growl of mock-outrage

and bit his nipple. "Ouch!" He grasped her wrist and they tussled enjoyably for a few moments before Anderton released her. "And I'm definitely too old for round two, right at this moment. Come on, let's get a drink."

They both heaved themselves off the floor, Kate groaning as loudly as Anderton did. "I'm thinking about taking yoga up again," she said, apropos of nothing except wondering when it was she got so inflexible.

Anderton was poking around in the wine rack over by the wall. "Hmm?"

"Never mind," said Kate. "I'm going to take a quick shower."

***

WHEN SHE CAME BACK DOWNSTAIRS, in her pyjamas and wrapped in her dressing gown, Anderton handed her one of his enormous wine glasses, half full of red wine. "I don't think I'm going to finish this," said Kate, faintly.

"I'll have the rest, don't worry." Anderton drew her down beside him on the sofa. "Now, how are things at work?"

As she told him what she could, Kate found herself thinking about what a refreshing change it was to have someone listen to *her* for a change. All the interviews and questioning and trying to tease out evidence and information from suspects; it meant you spent most of your days listening to other people speak. Perhaps that was why Anderton was such a good listener; he had years of experience.

"So, what exactly was it that bothered you about the Callihan crime scene?"

"That's just it," said Kate. "I don't know. You know I sometimes get those little bits of...of intuition, I suppose you'd call it."

"I do remember, yes."

"Well, it was one of those." Kate took a sip of her wine, looking down at the shimmering maroon surface in the glass. "Something intangible. I noticed something, but I don't know what I noticed."

"Well," said Anderton. "I also remember that, generally, these things tend to eventually come to you."

Kate smiled at him. "I know. I don't know why I always worry I won't be able to work out what it means when I normally do. I suppose I always think 'this is the one time I might *not* be able to get it'."

Anderton bent his head to hers and kissed her. "Well, I certainly wouldn't worry about it now."

"I won't."

Anderton took the glass from her hand and placed it on the coffee table. "And now, what do you say to round two?"

Kate kissed him back. "I say yes."

"In bed, though."

Kate laughed. "That too. Come on."

It wasn't until afterwards, when Anderton was already snoring, that Kate remembered her thought processes in the car driving over here. She rolled onto her back and stared up through the darkness at the unseen ceiling. *Was* she going to have that conversation with Anderton? Did she even want to? She pondered for a moment, swinging from one way of thought to another, before she yawned and rolled back on her side again. This wasn't the time to be thinking about the future. She needed to get some sleep.

Chapter Seven

AMANDA CALLIHAN'S SISTER WAS CALLED Mary Stirling, and she lived in a suburb of Edinburgh. By the time Kate spoke to her on the telephone, local police had broken the news of her sister's death to her and she sounded in control of herself, if understandably tearful. She sounded a nice woman, her voice softened by the hint of a Scottish burr.

"Manda was a lovely person, she really was. She was so soft-hearted. She's not had an easy life—it seems so cruel for it to be cut short like this—" Mary's voice broke in a sob. After a moment, when Kate could hear her taking deep breaths on the other end of the line, she came back on the phone. "How can I help you, DI Redman? I'm sorry."

Kate felt like she should be apologising to Mary. "We're trying to build up a picture of Amanda's life, Mrs Stirling, trying to see if there's anything we should know that might lead us to a suspect."

"I appreciate that—"

"When was the last time you saw or spoke to

Amanda?" Kate could hear Mary gulp. "Was it recently?"

"We normally spoke most weeks. I can't remember the last time exactly—och, yes, I can because Manda was planning on coming up to see us, and she wanted to check we'd be around. That must have been... Thursday, last week? Was it the fourteenth?"

Kate glanced at the little calendar she kept on her desk. "Yes, that's right, Mrs Stirling. Can you remember your conversation? How did Amanda sound?"

"Sound?"

"Did she sound worried or upset in any way? Did she mention anything that might have been bothering her?"

"I don't think so." Mary Stirling sounded unsure. Kate waited, not wanting to push her into making something up out of sheer nervousness, which had been known to happen occasionally. "No," said Mary, eventually, and more firmly. "She sounded fine, quite happy and quite excited at the thought of coming up here."

Kate nodded and asked more questions, about Amanda's family, her childhood, her relationships and her work. Mary was forthcoming but succinct, and yet again, Kate wished she was doing this interview face to face instead. You got so much more from being physically present at an interview. Would DCI Weaver authorise a trip up to Edinburgh so that Kate could interview Mary again, in more depth? *Come off it, Kate.* She wasn't even going to bother asking.

As she was on the verge of thanking Mary Stirling and ringing off, Kate remembered something. "You said she'd had a bit of a hard life, Mrs Stirling. What did you mean by that?"

Mary sounded a little defensive. "Oh, it was nothing, nothing much. It's just—I don't think life had worked out for Manda quite as she hoped it would. I mean, she always wanted a family, but she just never seemed to meet the right kind of man, not in time, anyway." Kate winced, glad she couldn't be seen. "And I told you she used to be a social worker, which she enjoyed but found really hard, and about ten years ago, she had a bit of a breakdown and had to leave. That's when she got into yoga and that sort of thing. Alternative health, I suppose you'd call it." Mary's voice was growing tearful again. "Och, and it's just so cruel and unfair that somebody's done this to her."

Kate soothed her without promising miracles. When she'd hung up the phone, she scribbled a note to herself; *look into background of victim esp. social work.* It probably had no bearing on what had happened, but you never knew...

Kate dropped her pen and pushed her chair back. It was quiet in the office, unusually, with both Chloe and Rav out interviewing witnesses. Theo was typing busily away at his computer. Kate pondered for a moment. Should she crack straight on with delving into Amanda Callihan's past? That would be slow and painstaking work, which was probably why it didn't much appeal. She decided to make herself and Theo a coffee as her usual method of procrastination.

Some mad impulse made her knock on DCI Weaver's door to offer her a hot drink. Even as she opened the door to the other woman's sharp 'enter'— what was wrong with saying 'come in', like every normal human being?—Kate wondered why she was bothering.

"I was just wondering if you wanted a coffee? I'm making one." Kate tried to sound as pleasant and as neutral as possible.

DCI Weaver looked up from the papers on her desk. She looked slightly less intimidating than normal—almost, Kate was surprised to note, happy. Relaxed, even. What was going on? "Thanks DS— sorry, *DI*—Redman. That would be nice. Black, no sugar."

Her tone was friendly enough to make Kate forgive her for the slip of the tongue. Maybe this time it really had been unintentional. "Coming right up."

"Oh, DI Redman, the PM for the Callihan case is coming up this afternoon. I'd like you to go."

"Really?" Kate couldn't help the note of surprise in her voice. Not that she minded attending post mortems, although it wasn't on her list of favourite ever tasks, but recently, it had always been allocated to someone else. "I mean, of course. What time is it?"

She made and distributed the drinks and returned to her desk with the details of the autopsy on a Post-it note. "What's going on with our Nicola, then?" she asked of Theo. "She's—dare I say it—almost human today."

Having known Theo for so long, Kate *knew* that this would be his chance to imply that Nicola's change in personality was something to do with sex. "In fact, Theo, I'll say it for you."

"What?" Theo looked puzzled.

"'She's just had a good seeing-to', ho, ho, banter banter. That's how it goes, isn't it?" Kate said, grinning.

Theo didn't smile. "What are you talking about?"

Kate felt foolish. "It's just—Nicola—oh, never mind." She swung back to face her desk, giving Theo a baffled look. What was up with *him*?

They worked in not quite comfortable silence for some minutes. Then, conscience getting the better of her, Kate asked "Are you okay, Theo?"

Theo looked up in surprise. "What, mate?"

"I asked if you were okay?"

Now it was Theo's turn to give her a baffled look. "I'm fine."

Kate wavered, wondering whether to probe deeper or not, and then gave up. "Okay."

Theo shook his head, but he gave her a grin that lightened the atmosphere a little. Kate caught sight of the clock and realised she'd have to leave if she was to make the post mortem on time.

It was a grey, nothing-weather sort of day, but not too cold for autumn. Kate kicked aside drifts of red and yellow leaves before she ran up the steps to the pathology laboratories. The doctor performing the post mortem was Andrew Stanton, a (very) old boyfriend of Kate's. She was still on friendly terms with him and his wife. Come to think of it, she owed them a dinner invitation. She remembered talking with Chloe in the car some days ago about a Halloween party. Well, she was damn well going to go ahead and have one.

"Do you and Juliet fancy coming to a Halloween party?" she asked, as they made their way to the theatre.

Andrew looked at her with surprise. "Ah—yes?" After a moment, he chuckled. "I didn't think those were your sort of thing, Kate."

"Well, not normally. I mean, I'm normally too busy, but I fancy one this year. So, you'll come then? And maybe bring some friends?" Thinking of Chloe, she added. "Preferably single ones."

Andrew looked even more surprised. "Single? But I thought you and DCI Anderton were—"

"Oh, we are, we are. I'm thinking of a friend of mine. But don't worry too much." Kate was regretting asking by now.

Luckily, Andrew was nothing if not professional and took his post mortems seriously. They dropped the chat as soon as they entered the room in which the body lay on the gurney, shrouded in dark green cloth. Kate took a seat over by the wall as Andrew scrubbed up.

Kate was used to Andrew working in silence, punctuated only by the occasional terse remark. She was free to think, turning her gaze away from the particularly gory bits. One part of her mind was on the proposed party; thinking of invitations and who to invite and what she was going to cook and where to get some decorations. And fancy dress, of course. What was she going to wear? The other half of her brain was attending the post mortem and thinking about the victim. Again, she felt that flash of unease about the crime scene—something she'd missed. What was it? Kate made a mental note to look at the crime scene photographs again when she was back in the office.

At length, Andrew finished stitching, straightened up and drew the sheet back over the body. He rolled his shoulders, shook his head and removed his gloves, throwing them in the hazardous waste bin by the sink.

"So?" asked Kate.

"Well, like I said earlier, she died from strangulation. But—and this may be significant—she was stunned by a blow to the head first."

"Really? She didn't put up a fight?"

"Not at all. There's nothing under her fingernails, there are no defence wounds."

"Interesting." Kate stared at the covered shape of

the body as if it might give her the answers. "Anything else pertinent?"

"She was a strong, healthy woman. Very fit for her age. She'd not had a child. Um, no sign of sexual assault." Andrew ran his hand through his hair, once red, now almost entirely grey. "What else?"

"It's fine," said Kate. "I can wait for the report now we've got the vitals."

"Okay. I'll have it over to you in a day or so, quick as I can."

"Thanks, Andrew." She raised a hand in farewell and turned to go. "Oh, Halloween party? It'll be on Halloween, ha, of course."

Andrew grinned. "We'll look forward to it. Um... these single friends you're looking for. Er, do they have to be male or female?"

Kate laughed. "Male. I'm pretty sure that's what she's looking for."

"Hmm. Well, I'll do my best."

Kate drove back to the station, feeling cheerful. Should she make the party a child-friendly one? It made it more likely that people would be able to come if they didn't have to worry about babysitters. Then she thought of Olbeck and Jeff's children and how timid and wary of strangers they were. Oh dear, perhaps not. The thought of subjecting two damaged children to a room full of scarily-dressed adults was not a good one. No, best keep it adults-only. Not to mention that it would actually be much more fun without little children there, thought Kate, who then felt slightly guilty. She put all thoughts of the party from her mind as she drove into the station car park and attempted to refocus on work.

Chapter Eight

THE NEXT MORNING WAS A little gift from heaven: bright sunshine, a blue sky wisped with white cloud and the autumn colours of the trees in full glorious colour. Kate almost bounded into the office and headed for her desk, keen to get started.

"All right, bird?" Chloe was already at her desk, pecking away at her keyboard.

"Morning, bird." Kate's fingers flew over her own keyboard with a clatter. "Anything I should know about?"

"Not much. We're still pulling CCTV from the streets around Amanda's flat. Someone will have to go through that with a fine-tooth comb."

Kate made a face. "Bagsy not me."

"I think Rav's on it. He's good at that." Chloe pushed her chair back a little, stretched and yawned. "God, I'm knackered already. How did the PM go?"

"I'm just emailing that round now." Kate signed off her email, making sure she'd copied in DCI Weaver as well as everyone else, and sent it. She remembered the time she'd genuinely forgotten to add Nicola's email to the 'To' column and boy, hadn't she heard about *that* for a week? Thinking of this, she quickly checked over her shoulder to see if Nicola was standing behind her—no—and turned back to Chloe. "By the way, how is our Nicola this morning?"

Chloe shrugged. "Haven't seen her yet. I don't think she's even in. Why?"

Kate told her about Nicola's rather nicer behaviour of yesterday. Chloe pulled a face. "About time. But no, I don't know why."

"Well, never mind." Kate tried to focus her mind on what she had to do. She consulted her notes. *Look into background of victim esp. social work.* Ah, yes. Was there something else she had to remember? What was it? She cudgelled her memory and remembered. Something about the crime scene photographs— that's right, she had to check them to see if she could put her finger on what exactly was making her uneasy.

She almost got up to do that right there and then but decided to do a bit of research on Amanda Callihan. Knowing the victim was sometimes the quickest and easiest route to their killer. She ran Amanda's name through various databases, checking on previous convictions, addresses, connections. No previous convictions. She could see from the electoral roll that Amanda had lived in her flat for ten years. Kate was beginning to think that she should go back there, to the scene of the crime. No doubt there was a plethora of information on Amanda to be found there, and Kate could also see if she could pinpoint what she'd felt was wrong. It would be much easier to do on the scene, rather than using a photograph. She made up her mind.

"I'm off to Amanda's flat," she told her friend. "Can you tell our Nicola if she asks?"

"Hopefully she won't. But, yes, I will. See you later, bird."

Kate blew her an airy kiss, picked up her coat and handbag, and strode from the office.

The beautiful weather held. It was almost warm, most un-October-like, thought Kate, swinging her car into a free space in the carpark by Amanda's flat. She wondered who would inherit it. Her sister, perhaps? Amanda's will was yet another thing to be looked into.

Blue and white crime-scene tape still garlanded the door. Kate ducked under it and unlocked the door. She waited in the small hallway for a moment, trying to clear her mind. Then she strode purposefully into the living room, trying to look at the whole room in one sweeping gaze.

This time, she saw it almost at once. The ornament – or statue, she supposed, would be a better term. On the top of a bookcase, half-hidden amongst vases and knick-knacks, stood the same winged statue of a woman that Kate had seen on the sideboard of Roland Barry's house.

Kate held her breath and let it out in a rush. Then she walked, almost tiptoeing, up to the bookcase, as if the statue might take flight if she were too rushed in her movements. Without touching it, Kate peered closer, checking she hadn't been mistaken. No, she hadn't—it was the same sort of statue. She reached for her bag and extracted a pair of gloves and an evidence bag. Once the object was safely stowed in the latter, Kate moved to the window and held it up to the light.

It seemed to be made of some sort of marble, or was it only plaster? Tests would show. Kate turned it slowly around. The little face of the woman was quite blank. Only vague outlines of facial features showed. The wings were more detailed. The woman's hair looked vaguely snake-like. Who was she supposed to be? Kate pondered. Medusa? That was the only goddess she could think of with snakes for hair. More research was needed.

Of course, it could be the case that this was complete coincidence. Perhaps both Roland Barry and Amanda Callihan had bought the same ornament. Who would be able to confirm that? A close relative would seem the easiest option. Kate called the office to get the number of Roland Barry's sister. Then she dialled the sister.

"A what, dear?" asked Mrs Cole, when Kate had finally got hold of her and explained the situation.

Kate repeated her description of the statue. "I was wondering if you'd ever seen it before at Dr Barry's house?"

"Oh, I haven't been to poor Roly's house in a long time. I couldn't have told you what was there or not."

Kate cursed, silently. "Is it the sort of thing your brother liked, Mrs Cole?"

Mrs Cole sounded doubtful. "I'm not sure. He was a classics scholar at university, so I suppose it's possible. He didn't really buy ornaments though. He was more of a one for paintings."

As she said that, Kate remembered the picture of the Lake District location on Roland Barry's wall. That was something else to look into.

She thanked Mrs Cole and ended the call. Then she hesitated, torn between wanting to continue the search in Amanda Callihan's house and wanting to head back to the office to start investigating this mysterious statue. After a moment's more thought, she pulled out her mobile and rang Chloe.

"Are you at the station?" she asked, once her friend answered.

"Yep. Why?"

Kate explained succinctly. "I could do with a hand here. I want to do a more thorough search, see if I can find anything that might link the two cases. Can you come?"

"What about the statue?"

"Well, it could be complete coincidence. I know we have to look into it, but it can wait for an hour or so."

"Weaver needs to know," warned Chloe.

"I know *that*. Look, bird, if you can get away, come and help me search, and then we'll head back together and give her an update." Kate thought for a moment and then added, smiling, "Safety in numbers, hey?"

Chloe laughed. "Okay. I'm on my way. Twenty minutes."

After she'd disconnected the call, Kate put the evidence bag with the statue by the front door with her handbag. Not that she was likely to *forget* it. She liked to be methodical in a house search; it appealed to the meticulous part of her nature.

She began in the bedroom. Amanda's bedroom had a sad air about it regardless of the fact its owner was dead. This was something more, Kate thought. Despite Amanda having a boyfriend, the room seemed indicative of a lonely soul. Perhaps it was the rather austere bed; white metal with little decorative flourish. Perhaps it was the functional bedlinen, the lack of books on the side table, the minimal wall decoration. No photos, no plants. Kate thought of her own bedroom, with its lavishly made-up bed (good bedlinen was a bit of a fetish of hers), the cushions, the throws, the lushly green peace lily that stroked her bedside table with its long leaves. And Merlin, of course, king of her bed. He didn't like it much when Anderton stayed over, although that didn't happen often. Kate was momentarily side-tracked. What would happen with Merlin if she and Anderton moved in together? Cats were not fond of moving, she'd heard.

Cross that bridge when you come to it, Kate. She dragged her mind back to the job and began the search.

Chapter Nine

Kate had reached the stage of unearthing boxes from beneath the bed when she heard the front door to the flat open. "Bird?" she called.

"It's me." A moment later, Chloe appeared in the doorway of the bedroom. "God, what a sad little place."

"I thought that too." Kate wriggled backwards and brushed dust from her hands. "It made me wonder, to be honest. Why does this place feel so...so gloomy? Amanda was fairly young, she was fit, healthy, she had a boyfriend, she had a good relationship with her sister. Why the...the sadness?"

"Sometimes all those things aren't enough." For a moment, Chloe looked grimmer than Kate would have liked. Her friend was attractive, intelligent and solvent, but somehow, successful romantic attachments seemed to elude her.

"Anyway," said Kate, hastily. "I think I need to look into her past life. She worked as a social worker for years, apparently, and then had some kind of breakdown and got out of it." Chloe was still regarding the austere little bedroom with a frown. "Should be a place to start, don't you think?"

"Yeah." Chloe was wearing brown leather gloves and pulled each one from her hands absent-mindedly before tucking them in her coat pocket, staring about the room. "Where's this bloody statue, then?"

Kate led her to the evidence bag in the hall. Chloe picked it up and regarded it from several angles.

"Hmm. You're right. It's the same as from the Barry house."

"It could be coincidence," said Kate, doubt edging her voice.

"It could." Chloe held the bag up again and turned it. The statue's blank little face regarded them. "But I've never seen anything like this for sale before. Have you?"

Kate shook her head. "No. I don't even know if it's a specific goddess, deity—whatever."

"I do." Chloe grasped the plastic of the bag and smoothed it over the statue's face. "It's an Erinyes."

"A *what*?"

Chloe glanced at her with a half-smile. "I did some Classics at university. The Erinyes are the Furies. Heard of them?"

Kate considered. "I think so. They're the—the punishing ones? Or the Fates?"

"Both." Chloe held up the statue again. The blank, black face swung back and forth like a pendulum, and Kate was conscious of a creeping unease. "The Furies were spirits of justice. Maybe vengeance, too. They had snakes for hair."

"I thought that was Medusa."

Chloe smiled. "Her too. It seemed to be the accessory for vengeful Greek goddesses."

Kate didn't smile. She looked at the empty gaze of the statue's little face. "*If* the killer left that here... is that what they're saying? This is vengeance? This is justice?"

Chloe looked at her. "Maybe."

The room seemed to chill for a moment. "Vengeance for what?" Kate murmured.

Chloe became brisk. "That's *if* the killer did leave it here. And at Barry's house. It could be a complete coincidence."

"We need to find out whether Amanda Callihan bought this statue. And where they were made."

"That would be a start."

"I'll ring Amanda's sister," said Kate.

"And I'll start researching the statue," said Chloe.

They headed for the door. "Hold on," said Kate, her fingers on the door knob. "Do we tell Nicola now, or what?"

Chloe's gaze met hers, mischevious in the way that Kate loved about her friend. "Oh, I don't think so, do you? Not yet, anyway. We've got nothing concrete."

"Roger that," said Kate, and they fist-bumped and headed off on their private missions.

Back in the office, Kate got hold of Mary Stirling quite easily and asked whether she knew if Amanda had bought or been given the Erinyes statue. Mary was clearly willing to help but the trouble was that she hadn't visited her sister's flat in several years. "Manda normally came up to us," Mary explained. "She loved to see the children, and she liked the countryside up here. Well, you can understand it, can't you? I never really liked her flat, I have to say, although obviously I never said anything. But she never seemed particularly comfortable there, it was funny—"

"The statue, Mrs Stirling?" Kate prompted.

"Oh, sorry. No, I don't *think* she had anything like that when I last went to see her. But I can't be exactly sure."

"No, I understand it's difficult."

Mary sounded as though she was thinking aloud. "It's... It's an odd thing for Manda to have bought, I have to say. Not her style at all."

That sounded more promising. Kate jotted down a few notes, listening to Mary speak. Then she realised that the victim's sister was probably the best person to ask about Amanda's background and career change. "Mrs Stirling—"

"Please, call me Mary."

"Thanks. Mary, you mentioned that Amanda had gone through a difficult time in her work, some years ago. When she was a social worker. Could you tell me about that?"

Mary's voice sounded troubled. "Oh, it's a few years ago now, but it was pretty bad. Manda had...well, she'd gone through quite a tough time at work. It's so hard being a social worker, so hard—you're blamed if you do too much, and you're blamed if you don't do enough. You just can't win."

"Can you be more specific?"

"Oh, well, poor Manda... She—she got embroiled in this bit of...well, it was a bit of a scandal. She said it was something to do with a child being killed. Something awful like that. The family were known to social services, and the little one should have been removed but wasn't, for some reason, and ended up dead. Awful. That's what Manda said, anyway. Of course, it wasn't her *fault,* but I think she blamed herself."

Kate was scribbling fast. "So, when and where was this, Mary?"

"Och, it was... Oh, when was it? Let me think. A long time ago now, before she moved to Abbeyford. Manda was working down in Whitehaven."

Kate wrote this down. Where was Whitehaven? Obviously south of Scotland or Mary wouldn't have used the word 'down'. A scandal involving the death of a child would have been headline news, if only in the local papers, but most likely it would have featured in the national dailies as well. Easy enough to check. She got a few more details out of Mary Stirling, thanked her, and said goodbye.

She looked up to see Theo looking over at her enquiringly. "Got something, mate?" he asked.

"I hope so. Need to do a bit more digging."

Theo nodded. Then he pushed his chair back from his desk and came over to her desk. Now it was Kate's turn to look at him enquiringly. "You okay?"

Theo looked diffident. "You up to anything after work, mate?"

Kate felt her eyebrows shoot up. She and Theo had socialised after work before, but not just the two of them. Surely, he wasn't suggesting a date? She looked at his face and decided that he wasn't. "Um, not sure." She had been due to see Anderton but her curiousity was piqued. "Why? Do you fancy a drink or something?"

"Yeah, that'd be great." Theo looked relieved. Burning with curiosity, Kate opened her mouth to ask him more but shut it again.

"Down the Arms?" she suggested. The Arms was actually called The King's Head, but it had been unofficially adopted by Abbeyford CID as a drinking place, hence its nickname of 'The Coppers' Arms'.

"Nah, not the Arms. Somewhere nicer."

"You aren't asking me out on a date, are you?" Kate asked, becoming paranoid again.

Theo scoffed. "As *if*, woman. Don't flatter yourself. Just thought it'd be nice to have a drink with my old pal."

"Less of the old," Kate said, grinning. "Okay, how about the Black Cat?"

"Sorted. Come and get me when you knock off."

Theo wandered back to his desk, hands in his

pockets and whistling. Kate, still slightly puzzled, shook her head and returned her attention to her work. She picked up the folder on the Barry case and leafed through it. *Could* there be a connection between the two cases? The statue or something else? Kate scribbled down idle thoughts. *Social work? Teaching institution? Roland—a client of Amanda's?* She tried to recollect the interview that they'd had with Roland Barry's cleaner, whether there had been anything that—what was her name again? Mrs Cuckoo? No, that couldn't be it. Kate checked the name and then slapped a hand to her forehead, groaning aloud.

"Kate?" Rav was passing her desk. "You okay?"

"I'm fine, Rav. I'm just an idiot."

If Rav had been Theo, he would have heartily concurred with this remark and probably elaborated on it at length. As it was, Rav smiled at her in a slightly puzzled way, patted her shoulder, and continued on his way.

Shaking her head at herself, Kate grabbed the folder and found Sandra Cuckfield's contact details. Why hadn't she thought of checking with Roland Barry's cleaner? Of *course* she would know whether the statue had always been there or whether it was something she'd not seen before. Kate pulled her desk phone over towards herself and dialled, eagerly awaiting a response.

Chapter Ten

KATE CALLED IT A NIGHT at seven o'clock. She had half expected Theo to take a rain check on their 'date'—he wasn't the most reliable in terms of keeping social appointments—but when she got up and began to gather her things about her, she could see he was still at his desk.

"Want that drink, then?"

"Yeah, mate. I'm bushed." Theo stretched his arms out behind his head and yawned. "Come on, first round is mine."

As they made their way to the door of the office, they passed DCI Weaver in the corridor. She gave them a fairly civil 'goodnight' as they walked by her, but Kate was aware of a frank curiosity in her glance. She felt rather uncomfortable, knowing the DCI knew of Kate and Anderton's relationship. Did Nicola think that she and Theo were—well, more than colleagues or friends? *Forget it, Kate. She hates you anyway so what do you care?*

Theo seemed in an unusually pensive mood. Kate found a table at the back of the bar, near the open fire, while Theo queued for drinks. As Kate waited, watching the flickering flames, she recalled all the other times she'd been there. The time that her then boyfriend Tin had asked her to go to America with him. Tin. Kate couldn't quite recall him with fondness, but she wished him well anyway. Wasn't he married now? Occasionally she came across his by-line in one of the national papers, but she'd never seen him since. She'd sat here with Olbeck often. Anderton too. Thinking of him, she pulled out her phone and tapped out a quick message. *Quick drink with Theo after work. He says hi. CU later x.* That should assuage any jealousy on Anderton's part. He wasn't prone to it, but then he knew of Theo's reputation.

Theo placed a glass of red wine in front of her and sat down opposite with his pint.

"Cheers," said Kate, clinking glasses.

"Cheers." Theo took a long pull and then put the glass down with a sigh. "So, what's new on the case?"

Kate mentally raised her eyebrows. So, he just wanted to talk work? Fine with her, but why here? "Bit of a breakthrough, actually. Nicola was going to debrief us tomorrow."

Theo leant forward. "Yeah? What?"

"The statue. It didn't belong to Roland Barry. The cleaning lady had never seen it before."

Theo pursed his lips in a silent whistle. "Right. Interesting."

"So, Rav's going to be all over that tomorrow.

Tracking down the manufacturer—or trying to. Seeing where it's sold."

Theo nodded. "You know what else we should do? Run a search on whether there's been any other recent murders with this statue at the crime scene."

Kate was impressed—and annoyed. She should have thought of that. "That's a good idea, Theo. You should run it past Nicola, but I'm sure she'll go for it."

"Yeah, I will." Theo's face darkened momentarily. "So, anyway, what else is new?"

They chatted for a few minutes about work, their cases, various news-worthy events. Kate fetched them a second drink, reminding herself that she'd have to leave the car at the police station and walk in the next morning. So no going to Anderton's then. She'd call him on the way home. Merlin would be pleased to see her, at least.

After they finished the second drink, Kate hesitated. Then, just as Theo was getting up for the third round, she asked, "Was there a particular reason you wanted to talk tonight, Theo?"

Again, she crossed her fingers that she hadn't misread the situation. Even if she hadn't been with Anderton, she'd learnt her lesson of not mixing business with pleasure. Good looking as Theo was, she just didn't feel that way about him.

Theo looked embarrassed, not hitherto an emotion Kate would ever have associated with him. "Well, you know, sometimes it's good to get a chick's opinion."

Kate rolled her eyes. "An opinion on what, Theo? Sewing? Pink fluffy things? Radical feminism?"

Theo grinned. "Nah, you know. It's just... Well, you and Anderton—" He broke off for a moment. "How long have you been together now?"

Kate had to think. "About a year, officially?"

"Officially?" Theo's grin grew wider. "So how long were the two of you sneaking around behind our backs?"

"I didn't mean that!" Kate heard the rising note in her voice and controlled it. "I just mean—oh, you know what I mean."

"Yeah. But, it's worked out for you, yeah?"

"So far," Kate said, cautiously. "Look, Theo, what is this about? Are you having girlfriend trouble?"

Theo scoffed. "As if. Nah, it's more... Well, what if you're not sure where it's going?"

With difficulty, Kate repressed a scream. "Who is this woman?"

"Never you mind."

For some reason, Chloe's face came into Kate's mind. Surely not? She opened her mouth to ask and then shut it again. "Look," she tried. "I want to help you, Theo, but this is something you've got to work out for yourself. What *you* want. And what she wants. See if you can meet in the middle, you know."

"Right," said Theo, with some finality. Kate got the message.

"Look, I'd better go."

"Yeah, okay. Think I'll stay for another."

Kate nodded and began gathering her belongings. "Oh, by the way. You're coming to the party, right?"

"Party?"

"My Halloween party. Next weekend? I did give you the invitation."

"Oh, that. Yeah, sure. Plenty of hot chicks going to be there, right?"

"Of course," said Kate, crossing her fingers out of sight under the table.

"Cool. See you tomorrow then, mate."

Kate clapped a hand on his shoulder in farewell and made her way to the door. As she shut it behind her, she could see Theo through the panes of glass. He was texting someone on his phone. This mystery lady? Kate shrugged and trotted down the front steps to the street.

As she walked home, she phoned Anderton on her mobile and related much of the conversation to him. "What do you think's up with him?"

Anderton sounded amused. "He's probably finally in love with someone who doesn't feel the same way about him. For a change."

Kate laughed. "Romantic karma."

"Well, quite. Anyway, enough about Theo. Shall I come on over or are you too tired?"

"Come on over. I'll try and stay awake."

Now it was Anderton's turn to laugh. "Do your best. I'll see you soon."

"Bye." Kate put the phone back into her handbag and strode off into the night, hands in her pockets.

Chapter Eleven

As Kate had predicted, DCI Weaver held an incident room debrief the next morning. Kate rubbed her eyes as she listened. Although she'd only had two glasses of wine the night before, the resulting late night of love-making with Anderton meant she'd had far too little sleep. She yawned, and Chloe, leaning on the desk beside her, caught it. Kate expected DCI Weaver to pull them both up on it, make some sort of pointed remark, but she didn't. Nicola looked rather exhausted herself. Looking around the room, Kate thought that everyone was looking rather wiped out. Complex murder cases had that effect on you. Added to that the time of year, with the seasonal round of colds and flu, and the weather turning grim, grey and blustery, and it was hardly surprising that nobody was looking their best.

DCI Weaver came to a halt before the two whiteboards covering both cases. "So, to recap. The statue links the two cases, and it's imperative that we find out how and why this might be. I want you all to concentrate your attention on finding out more about it. DC Cheetam, you'll be researching possible manufacturers, retailers, where these statues originate from."

She turned slowly on one high heel, examining the boards as if in thought. "DS Wapping, DI Redman, I want you to do a deep dive on the history of both Roland Barry and Amanda Callihan. Find out if anything else other than the statue links them. Interview their relatives, their work colleagues, find out everything you can." She ran a hand over her glossy hair, in a way that meant Kate was suddenly reminded of Anderton doing exactly the same. Was it something they taught you at Chief Inspector level? "Now, we're still waiting on a lot of the forensic reports. DS Marsh, you made a very good suggestion as to whether there have been any other cases in which this statue has been found." Theo looked smug. "Could you take on that task?"

"Sure." Looking for similarities in differing murder cases was something of a speciality of Theo's. Kate remembered how he'd managed to track down a link between cases in the butterfly killer case, all those years ago. Her stomach twisted. Was this another serial killer? Surely not? But what if it was?

Dismissed by their DCI, Kate and Chloe made their way back to their desks.

"So, bird, you want to take Roland or Amanda? I'm easy."

"I'll do Amanda." Kate had already had contact

with Amanda's sister and knew that it would make things a little easier. "If that's okay with you."

"No problem. I'll get us a coffee."

When Chloe returned with two steaming mugs, Kate took one from her and sat back in her chair in thought. Amanda Callihan. Social worker turned yoga teacher. Which strand of her career to unpick first? There was the case that her sister had mentioned, the one in Whitehaven, The child that should have been removed from her family for safety but hadn't been, with tragic results. A depressingly common story. Should she start there? Kate thought of the mounds of data she would have to wade through, the newspaper headlines to look up, the phone calls to people she didn't know, the answerphone messages she would have to leave that might or might not be returned. Inwardly, she groaned. If she'd been feeling more awake, that might have been the place to start. But, fogged with tiredness as she was, she decided to get a bit of fresh air instead.

"I'm off to the yoga centre where Amanda worked," she told Chloe, as was the protocol for all officers at Abbeyford when going somewhere alone. Chloe merely nodded; she was already on the phone chasing leads of her own.

***

AS KATE STEPPED OUTSIDE, SHE was almost blown off her feet by the howling wind. Clutching her wildly flapping coat around her, hair whipping across her face, she battled across the car park and slammed the car door thankfully. Well, there was fresh air at least... The sky was an odd yellowish-grey colour and the gale was tearing the last of the autumn leaves from the trees. Kate turned on the car radio to hear the weather forecaster promising a storm across Wales and the South West. *Great*. Kate looked up the address of Amanda Callihan's place of work, put the car in gear, and drove away.

Namaste Studios were located up a tiny cobbled side street in the centre of Abbeyford. Parking was impossible. Cursing, Kate drove around until she found a council car park and noted down the parking money amount in her notebook to claim back on expenses later. Anderton had once laughed at her careful notes of what she'd run up in expenses but, as she pointed out rather acerbically to him, he earned a great deal more money than she did. He had had the grace to look a little sheepish at that.

Kate reached the door of the studios, which was set back from the street. The rooms were located in a tall, Georgian building. *Namaste Studios* was neatly printed by the doorbell, under *R. Brown, Life Coach* for the doorbell above. Kate pressed the bell and waited for a response.

She was granted entry and climbed the stairs. The walls were painted a serene pale blue, and she could smell some sort of incense as she wound her way upwards. On the second floor, the corridor opened out into a reception area, clean and white, with a pretty, dark-haired girl sat behind the desk. The girl looked at her with an apologetic smile. "I'm sorry, but the midday class has started," she said.

"Oh, I'm not here for a class." Kate produced her credentials and the girl's dark blue eyes widened. "I'm investigating the death of one of your instructors, I'm afraid. Amanda Callihan?"

Those blue eyes filled with tears. "Oh, Amanda," the girl said and burst into sobs.

The next few minutes were taken up with Kate attempting to soothe the girl—Josie Hill, according to her name tag—back into some sort of sense. As she tried to get the girl to stop crying, Kate heard some sort of Eastern music coming from the studio nearest the desk. There was a glass panel in the studio door, and Kate could see several women bending and contorting themselves on purple mats on the white-painted floor.

At last, Josie got herself under control. "I'm sorry," she gasped, "but it's just so awful. It was such a shock to us all."

"I'm sure it was. I'm so sorry," said Kate. She handed Josie another tissue—she always carried several packets around in her handbag. "I was hoping you might be able to help me?"

"I'll try," said Josie, with a watery sniff. Kate wondered at her age. Surely no more than twenty-two?

"When does the next class start, Josie?" Kate didn't want a whole load of lycra-clad women descending on them in the middle of the interview.

"Not until three. The instructors have a lunch break after the midday class."

"Great. Now, as I mentioned before, I'm investigating Amanda's—" Kate had been about to say 'murder' but decided on a euphemism, in case Josie started crying again. "I'm investigating Amanda's case. We're trying to piece together her history, the kind of person she was, her friends and anyone she knew that might be significant. What can you tell me about her?"

For all her youth and soft-hearted nature, Josie turned out to be quite observant. Kate learnt that Amanda had worked for the studio for three years and was "nice, but, like, quite self-contained." Josie, warming to her theme while the tears dried on her cheeks, said "She always seemed a little...sad, maybe, if that's the word. Not, like, *sad*, like pathetic, more— more she just seemed a bit..."

Kate always tried not to prompt but the silence stretched out so long that she couldn't help saying "Lonely?"

Josie looked at her gratefully. "Yeah, lonely, maybe. I mean, she always would come out for a drink and come to the Christmas party and stuff. She wasn't anti-social, but she was... I suppose she was a bit of an introvert, really."

"What about her family? Did she have a partner?"

Josie crumpled up her mouth as she pondered. "She had a sister, she was close to her sister, always going up to Scotland to visit her. She was seeing this bloke, I can't remember his name, but he was quite new. She hadn't been seeing him for long." Something seemed to occur to her and she gulped. "Oh my god, it wasn't *him*, was it? It's always the men, isn't it?"

"I'm afraid I can't comment on that, Josie," Kate said gently. She scribbled down a few more notes and asked a few more questions.

As her conversation with Josie drew to a close, she was aware of the music stopping and bustle and hum of people beginning to pack up after their yoga class. "Josie, thanks for your time, it's been really helpful. I'd like to talk to the instructors now, if they're free?"

"I'll check for you," Josie said and scurried into the studio while Kate moved out of the way of the stream of flushed and sweaty women pouring past her on the way to the changing rooms.

After her interview with the yoga teacher, Dawn Hassan, which yielded little other than much of what Josie had already told her, Kate thanked both women again. She said goodbye and went back out into the corridor, wondering where to go from there. She had a name from Dawn, one of Amanda's friends who she'd introduced to her work colleagues after her friend had come to a class. Kate read the name again: Charlotte Simpson. She would surely be the next best person to contact.

Kate ran down to the first floor landing, rounded the corner of the stairs and nearly ran into another woman who was walking up them. They both apologised simultaneously.

"Oh, sorry!"

"Sorry—"

Both laughed. "My fault entirely," said Kate.

"These stairs *are* rather narrow," said the woman. In the dim light of the hallway it was hard to make her out properly, but she looked to be in her late thirties, possibly older. She was thick-set, dressed in a rather frumpy woollen dress, sage-green and voluminous, under a beige parka. She didn't look much like a yoga student, and Kate wasn't surprised when the woman, smiling politely as she passed her, produced a key to the door on the landing that had a sign on the wall outside, *R. Brown, Life Coaching Services*.

Kate turned to go and then turned back on impulse. "Ms Brown?"

The woman looked surprised. "Yes?"

Kate introduced herself and why she was there.

Ms Brown's face contracted briefly. "Oh, God, yes. Poor Amanda. It was just too cruel. Too cruel for words."

"Did you know her?"

"Not well. I knew her to say hello to, like I do all the women here." Ms Brown hesitated for a moment and added, "Amanda *was* a client of mine, for a very brief time. She only came for one or two sessions."

"Would you mind if we had a quick chat, Ms Brown? I'm just trying to get as much information as I can on Amanda's background, and it would be so handy if you could give me anything—anything at all."

Ms Brown smiled sadly. "Of course. Of course, I will." She glanced at her watch, a fussy silver one with lots of curlicues.. "I've got a client coming in half an hour, but I can spare twenty minutes or so."

"Thank you."

Ms Brown unlocked her door and stood back to let Kate walk through. "I'm Rachel, by the way. Do come in."

Chapter Twelve

Rachel Brown's suite of rooms consisted of a large sitting room, where Kate now stood, with what looked like a tiny kitchenette off to one side and another door that possibly led to a bathroom or was perhaps only a store cupboard. The walls were magnolia woodchip, the carpet a sad brown, covered with a fluffy rug that Kate recognised as one from Ikea (she had one herself in her bedroom). There were a few indifferent watercolours of flowers and trees dotted about on the walls and a three piece suite in a faded floral pattern. Over by the window was a desk with a laptop, a white Buddha statue beside it and an incense burner the only other objects on it. A small filing cabinet on top of it. The whole set up reminded Kate rather oddly of Amanda's flat, in that it was tired and shabby, with that indefinable air of sadness permeating it.

Rachel, who appeared unembarrassed by her surroundings, headed to the filing cabinet, opened it and began flicking through the contents. "Amanda,

Amanda," she muttered, and then looked enquiringly at Kate. "What was her surname again?"

"Callihan. Amanda Callihan."

"Right. Oh, here we are." She extracted a slim cardboard file and then, gesturing for Kate to sit down on the sofa, took the opposite armchair. "Here we are." She withdrew a few sheets of paper from the folder. "Like I said, she only came for one session. No, sorry, two. Just two." Rachel bit her unpainted lip for a moment. "Normally, I obviously wouldn't give this to anyone to read. I take client confidentiality seriously. But the poor woman's dead, after all."

She handed Kate the two sheets of paper, clipped together.

"May I take this?" asked Kate. "I'd give you a receipt of course."

Rachel waved a hand. "It's fine. It's of no use to me now, and if you think it would help..."

Kate thanked her and carefully folded the papers away in her handbag. "Now, Mrs—Rachel, could you tell me anything else about Amanda?"

Rachel sat back in the armchair, her fingers tapping against the arm rests. "I'm not sure. There's so little I actually remember. It was well over a year ago she came to see me." She looked at Kate as if something had just occurred to her. "Oh, I'm sorry, I didn't even offer—would you like a cup of tea?"

Kate was parched but she didn't want the woman to get side-tracked. Besides, if the décor was anything to go by, the tea would most likely be herbal and taste of nothing more than faintly fruit-flavoured water. "No, thanks, Rachel. Anything you can remember about Amanda would be so helpful."

Rachel looked down at her lap for a moment. "She was unhappy. I'd say very unhappy. She used to work as a social worker, I assume you know that?" Kate nodded. "Well, she said she had to resign because of—well, actually I think she was signed off sick because she had some sort of breakdown. Something to do with a case she'd been involved in."

Kate nodded again. "Yes, that's something we're looking into."

Rachel looked troubled. "She came to me because she said she wanted to know what to do with her life. That's something I help with, you know, helping people figure out what it is they might like to do. Particularly after a difficult period in their lives—you know, after a divorce or a redundancy or an illness." Kate smiled encouragingly. "Well, there was that but... it was odd, but I got the impression she was scared of something."

Kate's internal sensor pricked up its ears. "Scared?" she asked.

Rachel nodded, looking even more troubled. "Yes. As I said, she only came twice. The second time, I was pushing her a little bit more about her past work experience and what have you, and she said something like 'I want to leave the past behind me, it's got nothing but bad memories, and I'm scared that one day it'll catch me up."

Kate stared. "She said that?"

"I know. That's why I remember it, it made a real impression on me." Rachel recited as if from memory. "'I'm scared that one day it'll catch me up.'"

The two women looked at one another. Kate was first to break eye contact, and she took out her notebook and wrote down what Rachel had just told her. "Anything else?"

Rachel shook her head. "That was her last session with me. The next week she rang to cancel, and I didn't see her again. Well, not in a professional capacity."

"Right." Kate wanted some time to mull over what Rachel Brown had told her. She also wanted to find out exactly what had happened in the case that cost Amanda Callihan her career. "I'll give you my card, Rachel. Please do contact me if you remember or think of anything else."

"Yes, of course." Rachel got up to usher Kate out and held out her hand to shake goodbye. She had a surprisingly strong handshake for someone who looked so, well, woolly. "Goodbye."

Kate battled her way back through the wind, mini-tornadoes of autumn leaves assaulting her as she opened the car door. As she subsided, gasping in relief, onto the driver's seat, a woman passed the front of the car, carrying a shopping bag in one hand and a jaunty orange pumpkin in the other. Kate was reminded that her Halloween party was in two days' time and she hadn't done any food shopping, decoration preparation or, indeed, house cleaning. She ripped a page from her notebook and scrawled down a list of things she needed to do. Hopefully, she'd be able to get away from work on time tonight, providing no great breakthrough had been achieved on either case. At least her costume was sorted; Kate had ordered it from Amazon a week ago. Two, in fact. "Zombie bride or sexy witch?" she mused to herself, reversing out of the car parking space and heading back to the office. "That is indeed the question."

The office was quiet when Kate returned; Rav sat at his computer, frowning and tapping at his keyboard. Theo was in DCI Weaver's office—Kate had seen them discussing something quite animatedly as she'd passed the glass wall of Nicola's office. She hoped that it was because Theo had found something in the historic cases database that might indicate a link to the present crimes. Then she remembered all the preparation she had to do for her party and, rather guilty, hoped he hadn't.

"Hey, Rav. How's it going? Anything?"

Rav looked up and sighed. "Absolutely nothing so far. I can't find a single manufacturer or a retail outlet that sells these things." He indicated the evidence photograph of the statue that lay next to his keyboard. "I'm wondering whether it was foreign-made."

"That's a possibility." Kate gave silent thanks that it wasn't her who had to do all this tedious but necessary research. "What else is there?"

Rav shrugged. "Dunno. Anyway, I'm going snow-blind here. Want a coffee?"

"Yep. Have a break."

They went over to the kitchen area at the back of the room and Rav filled the kettle.

"You still okay to come over on Saturday?" Kate asked, crouching down to try and find her favourite mug in the cupboard.

"Yeah, sure. It'll just be me, though."

Kate glanced up in surprise. "Oh. Jarina not feeling well?"

Rav looked both shy and proud. "Well, actually, I wasn't going to say anything yet, but...she's pregnant."

Kate leapt up with a cry. "Rav! That's fantastic news. Oh, that's brilliant, I'm thrilled for you." She gave him a hug. "Fabulous news."

"Thanks," Rav said, sounding both pleased and embarrassed. "Keep it to yourself though, yeah? Please, Kate? We didn't want to tell anyone 'til we've had the twelve-week scan."

"Of course, I won't say anything. When's the scan?"

"Next week."

Kate gave him another hug. His slender frame felt delicate beneath her arms and she thought, how funny, Rav's going to be a father. He only really seems like a boy himself still.

"I'm sure everything will be fine. But, of course I won't say anything, you have my word."

"Thanks," Rav said gratefully, and they made their coffees and returned to their desks.

Kate attempted to bring her attention back to the

job, but every so often she glanced up and gave Rav a conspiratorial smile and once, a little thumbs up. Then, with the sound of Theo and Nicola approaching the room, she hastily returned her attention to the computer and began the search for the case which had so badly affected Amanda Callihan.

Chapter Thirteen

KATE OPENED THE DOOR TO Anderton that night at about ten o'clock, having spent the previous three hours in frantic preparation for Saturday's party. Now, the house was festooned with black and orange paperchains, spider-web bunting hung from the stairs and no less than three giant pumpkins, grinning manically, adorned the porch. Space had been cleared in the kitchen cupboards for the Ocado delivery, and Kate had had to put several bottles of wine outside the back door, as she'd run out of room in the fridge.

"Blimey, what happened to you?" asked Anderton, proffering a bottle of red and a pizza box.

Kate caught sight of herself in the hallway mirror and groaned. She was hollow-eyed, greasy-haired and filthy. "I thought I'd demonstrate my Halloween costume early."

Anderton chuckled. "And there was me thinking you were going for the hot vampire look."

"I think that might be a contradiction in terms." Kate kissed him and shut the front door behind him.

As she did, the wind blew a handful of dead leaves into the hallway. "Damn."

"Leave them. They look quite atmospheric," Anderton said, glancing around at the decorations. "Now, why don't you sit down and I'll sort us out something to eat."

"Don't mess up the kitchen too much," warned Kate, but she staggered gratefully into the sitting room and slumped down on the sofa.

She watched the flicker and glimmer of the logs in the fireplace, half-dozing whilst listening to the comforting sounds of Anderton moving about in the kitchen. Merlin, looking suitably spooky, came in and jumped onto the sofa to curl up on her stomach.

"Kate. *Kate*."

"Mmmm?" Kate dragged her eyes open to see Anderton holding out a plate of pizza and salad. "Oh, thanks."

"Try and stay awake to eat it." Anderton sat down at the end of the sofa and pulled Kate's feet onto his lap.

"Don't rub my feet or I've got no chance." Kate hauled herself into a sitting position, dislodging an indignant Merlin, and tried to wake up.

"Busy day, then?"

"When isn't it?" Kate tried to avoid talking with her mouth full, but she was too ravenous for politeness.

"Any breakthrough yet?"

Kate swallowed a mouthful of pizza. "I'm looking

into Amanda Callihan's past. Something happened up north, in Whitehaven. I was reading all about it all afternoon." She stopped talking for a moment. "Hang on a minute—"

Anderton waited expectantly. Kate thought for a minute. What was it about Whitehaven that had rung a bell?

"That's it," she said slowly, thoughts becoming clear. "Whitehaven's in the Lake District, isn't it?"

"Last I heard."

"Well, then," said Kate. "Roland Barry had two pictures of somewhere in the Lake District in his house. What if that's another connection?"

Anderton nodded. "Something to look into, definitely. Run it past DCI Weaver tomorrow."

Kate groaned. "Fat chance of her letting me poke around up there." She swallowed the last mouthful on her plate. "God, I needed that."

"You need sleep. Go on, go up and get some rest. I'll clean up down here."

Kate gave him a grateful kiss and headed upstairs. She fell asleep almost as soon as her head hit the pillow.

The next day dawned cold but bright, a crisp autumn day where the sunlight touched the last of the brightly coloured leaves still clinging the branches of the trees. Kate, rejuvenated by a good night's sleep for once, drove to work feeling cheerful. She had a good sense of where she could go next in her investigations, and she had the party to look forward to tomorrow.

"You're coming to the party, aren't you?" she enquired of Theo as they made their morning coffee.

"Yeah, course I am, mate. Any hot single friends of yours going?"

"Oh, God, not you as well."

Theo looked puzzled. "What's the problem?"

Kate recollected herself. "Oh, nothing. What are you dressing up as?"

"It's a surprise."

Kate laughed. "You haven't even got a costume, have you?"

"I *said*, it's a surprise," Theo said, grinning. He flung his teaspoon into the kitchen sink. "Are we all going?"

"Yes, I think so. Mark's going to try and get a babysitter."

"What about Nicola?"

Kate blinked. The thought of asking DCI Weaver hadn't even crossed her mind. "Er... I don't know."

Theo frowned. "Have you even asked her?"

"Er—no." Kate felt a little jab of shame. It *was* a bit mean of her to have invited everybody bar one. "I—I didn't think it would be her thing."

"She's not as bad as you think, you know."

"Right." Kate squared her shoulders. "I'll go and ask her now."

She left her coffee in the kitchenette and

marched towards Nicola's office, groaning inwardly, both at Nicola's anticipated sharp refusal and the uncomfortable feeling that Kate had behaved badly by not including her. Kate blew out her cheeks and knocked at DCI Weaver's door, which was as firmly shut as always.

"Hello," Kate said, rather awkwardly on being asked to enter. DCI Weaver looked up without expression. "I'm—I just wondered... I'm having a Halloween party at my place tomorrow, and I just wondered whether you'd like to come? Sorry about the—" She bit off what she was going to say about the lateness of the invitation. *Don't make it worse, Kate.*

DCI Weaver looked blank for a moment. Then she smiled— a small smile but a definite one—and said, "That's kind of you to ask, DI Redman, but I'm—I'm afraid I have plans."

"Right! Right, no problem, completely understand. I just thought I'd ask—" Kate said, nodding and smiling. She said "Right," a few more times and backed out of the office, feeling like all kinds of an idiot.

She hurried back to her desk to immerse herself in work. Chloe looked up as she flung herself into her chair. "Did you get anything on Amanda Callihan's past?"

"I certainly did." Kate grabbed the folder which contained the various newspaper reports she'd tracked down online. "Awful case. I vaguely remember it, actually."

"What happened?"

Kate grimaced. "The usual sad story. A child was being abused and neglected, social services got involved but not soon enough and didn't do a very good job." She extracted one of the photocopies. "The little girl was called Kayla Scott. She was born to a teenage mother, Emma-Jane Scott, and social services were involved from the start because of the mother's age. Everything seemed okay. Emma-Jane got a lot of support from her mother, apparently, but then she, Emma-Jane, I mean—met this guy and things went downhill from there."

Chloe took the photocopied sheet and read it, her mouth turning down. "Let me guess, the baby starts showing signs of abuse."

"Yes. The grandmother—what was her name? Oh yes, Linda Scott. She started pressuring Emma-Jane to give Kayla to her for adoption, or fostering or something. Emma-Jane didn't want to; they had a massive falling out, social services were going to take the child into care."

Chloe had read to the end of the sheet, and sighed. "And before that could happen, Kayla died."

"Yes, a suspicious death but because of various things, the case against the bloke, Jay Greeling, collapsed and he walked free. The police didn't charge Emma-Jane with anything."

"Why not?"

Kate shrugged. "Lack of evidence, I suppose. They

bungled the original investigation, no two ways about it. Linda Scott made a number of threats against the social workers in the case and was cautioned. I think she was even going to try and sue them but gave up or thought better of it." Kate sat back down and propped her chin on her hands, looking across at Chloe. "So, a defenceless little girl dead and a bloody balls-up from start to finish."

"And, presumably, one of the social workers on the case was Amanda Callihan?"

"Yes."

"Was she the officer overseeing the whole thing?"

Kate shook her head. "No, not at all. That's why it's a bit odd. She was quite junior."

Chloe frowned. "Yet supposedly this was enough to make her give up her job entirely and move away." She looked down at the paper again. "These threats that the grandmother made. What were they?"

"Death threats, I suppose, of a sort." Kate ran a finger down the paper, trying to find the right line. "'I'll kill you for letting him get away with it'. That sort of thing."

"Hmm."

Kate leant back in her chair. "I'm going to talk to the officers involved up in Whitehaven. See what they say, whether they thought she was serious or not."

"How old would she be now. Linda Whatsit?"

Kate shrugged. "It was ten years ago so she would

be...hang on...sixty or something. Not that old. She had Emma-Kate young herself."

"Would a sixty-something woman be capable of both these crimes?"

Kate spread her hands. "I have no idea. That's what I'm going to find out."

"Good luck, bird." Chloe turned back to her computer. "Ooh. Party time tomorrow, isn't it?"

"Certainly is."

"I'm looking forward to it." Chloe looked at Kate with a grin. "Any fit single men coming?"

"Loads," said Kate, crossing her fingers under the table.

Chloe looked surprised but pleased. "Now I'm really looking forward to it."

Kate laughed. "Good. Right. I've got to get on."

Chapter Fourteen

THAT SATURDAY NIGHT, KATE OPENED the door to Anderton, her first guest, and gave a cry of disappointment.

"Where's your costume?"

"I'm wearing it," said Anderton, stepping into the house and kissing Kate.

"But you're just wearing a suit."

Anderton grinned. "Ah, but I'm dressed as a serial killer, right? And they go about looking just like everyone else."

Kate gave him a look. "Is that in the best possible taste, given the line of work we're in?"

Anderton laughed out loud. "It's *Halloween*. It's not supposed to be tasteful."

"Oh, well." Kate took a hopeful look out into the street for more guests, but none were forthcoming. "I'll get you a drink."

"You look very nice, by the way." Anderton held out a bottle of red wine. "Although possibly the green face is a step too far. Nice wig, though."

Kate giggled. "I've got to watch it near the candles,

it's extremely flammable." She scratched her head. "And itchy."

"Well, you witches have to suffer for beauty." Anderton made his way into the living room and stood, taking it all in. "My God. You really have gone all out haven't you? Are those dead leaves on the floor?"

"Yes. That was your idea."

"I didn't mean carpet the whole bloody house in them."

Kate handed him a drink. "They look good."

"Hmm. Well, I suppose they'll mop up the vomit, later."

The doorbell rang and Kate hurried to answer it, holding her pointy black hat on her head. The new guests turned out to be Andrew and Juliet Stanton and no less than three unaccompanied men, all of which, as Kate summed up in a lightning glance, might do for Chloe. She hugged Juliet and then Andrew and whispered, "Good work," in his ear.

"Come in, guys. Come and have a drink."

Andrew was wearing a long black cloak and struggling to keep a pair of false vampire teeth in his mouth. He spat them into his palm, laughing. "Well, I tried."

"Go on through." Kate asked Juliet what she would like to drink and ushered them into the living room. Andrew looked pleased to see Anderton. Kate heard the doorbell ring and hurried to open it, finding a large werewolf on the doorstep with a six-pack in one hairy paw.

"It's me," said Theo's muffled voice.

"Nice costume," Kate said, stepping back to let him come in. "Saves me from having to look at your face."

Theo slapped her bottom as he walked past, causing Kate to shriek. "That's sexual assault now, you know," she called after him, shaking her head as she turned to greet the guests she'd spotted coming up the path.

***

BY TEN O'CLOCK, THE HOUSE was full, and Kate was starting to feel pleasantly tipsy. She'd stuck to the fairly lightweight punch she'd made (although she had spotted Theo emptying a bottle of vodka into it at one point) and had some of the pumpkin soup that Chloe had brought with her.

"About time the dancing started," Anderton said, passing her in the hallway and giving her a kiss.

"Just don't let Rav commandeer the CD player. We'll be listening to hardcore grime all evening."

"Great party!" said someone who Kate didn't recognise for a moment, before realising it was one of the Stanton's guests. She smiled back.

The noise from the living room and kitchen was so loud that Kate barely heard the doorbell go again. Puzzled, for almost everyone she remembered inviting was already here, she opened the door to find Nicola Weaver on the doorstep, holding a bottle of champagne and smiling rather defensively.

"Oh," said Kate in genuine surprise. Then she got hold of herself. "Hello, DCI Weaver. Glad you could make it."

"My—those plans I had—they kind of fell through, so I thought—" Nicola thrust forward the champagne bottle.

"Sure, sure, nice you came along." Kate was conscious of an emotion she'd never before associated with DCI Weaver. It was pity. There hadn't been any other plans, she knew that now. She also knew that if Nicola realised that Kate pitied her, there would be hell to pay. "Come on in," she said loudly and casually, and let Nicola make her own way into the party. She followed her into the living room and, rather gleefully, clocked the brief look of horror that flashed across Chloe's face as she saw her DCI come into the room. Theo still had his wolf-mask on, so gauging his reaction was impossible.

Anderton came forward to offer Nicola a drink and began to chat to her. Chloe stalked towards Kate.

"You didn't tell me you'd invited her," she said, in what was supposed to be a whisper but had to be pitched rather louder because of the noise.

"Oh, come on, I could hardly leave her the only one not invited," Kate said, guiltily recalling that she'd done exactly that.

Chloe rolled her eyes. "Well, *I'm* not going to be talking shop."

"Me neither. Let's find you a hot bloke." Kate looked about the room, searching for Andrew and his party. She couldn't spot them. "My mate Stuart's coming later but he's married. Shame, he would have been right up your street."

"So, why tell me about him?" said Chloe grumpily as they wandered towards the kitchen. "I need another drink."

The doorbell went yet again, and Kate hurried to answer it. She opened it to see Olbeck standing there, with a giant plastic knife apparently sticking out of his head.

"It's a strong look," said Kate, laughing and hugging him.

"That's what I thought." Olbeck handed her a bottle of wine. "Sorry Jeff couldn't make it too, but we didn't want to get a babysitter."

"It's fine. I understand. Come on in."

She walked with him to the living room where Anderton spotted him and yelled "Mark!" with a note of pure delight in his voice. Kate smiled as she watched her friends and fellow officers standing in her living room. All of them finally back together again. It was a good feeling.

The party went on until the early hours, which Kate counted as a success. She'd avoided having her neighbours complain about the noise by inviting them, although Janet had only managed two small glasses of wine and left at about ten thirty. Quite respectable for an eighty year old though, thought Kate. She and Anderton had fallen into bed at about 3am, far too drunk to shag, and now, the next morning, were nursing their hangovers with bacon sandwiches and strong coffee.

"This is the worst part of parties," said Kate, groaning at the state of her house. "Clearing up afterwards.

"I'll help," said Kate's friend Hannah, who'd been the only one to stay the night as she lived too far away to get back the previous evening.

Kate smiled at her. "Thanks, Hannah."

Hannah flopped onto the available sofa with a sigh. "God, I'm getting too old for parties."

"Don't be daft. Look at my neighbour, Janet. She's eighty and she came dressed up as a pumpkin."

"True. It was good to see Jay and Laura again, it's been ages."

"I know," sighed Kate. She was close to her brother and his wife but over the last few years, she'd barely seen them. They lived busy lives in London and she—well, when did she ever really have the time to do anything?

Anderton heaved himself to his feet with a groan. "Right, let's do this. Get rid of these bloody leaves for a start." He kicked out at them with a rustle. "Ouch. My head." He looked wistful for a moment. "It *was* good to see everyone again. Be back with the team."

Kate half-smiled. Was now the time to suggest

that, if he missed it so much, he might want to return to work? Would he be able to, though? She looked across at Hannah, who was sitting back with her eyes closed, and decided against it. That was a conversation for another time.

"Come on," she said, getting up herself. "Brooms at the ready. Us witches always have plenty of brooms."

Chapter Fifteen

"So, who did you disappear off with then?"

Chloe, sitting across from Kate, looked smug. "His name is Roman."

"*Roman*?" Kate considered. "Interesting but... good. I like it. Was he the dark one?"

"Yep. With the beard."

Kate nodded. "Impressive, nice work. Are you seeing him again?"

Chloe looked even more smug, if it were possible. "Got a date tomorrow."

"I'm proud of you, bird." Kate held up a fist in solidarity. "I am definitely considering this party a success." She grinned at her friend, who winked back. "Now, let us turn our attention off this enjoyable subject and back onto work."

She took a long pull of coffee and regarded her to-do list. Whitehaven, that was the first thing. She brought up the telephone number and began to dial. Then, a thought occurring to her, she put down the receiver and hurried over to Rav's desk.

"Rav, hi. Any luck with finding the manufacturer of that statue yet?"

Rav looked up. "No, not yet. I'm trawling the internet though. Why?"

Kate pulled up a convenient chair and sat down. "It just occurred to me on the way to work. What if it's homemade? I mean, somebody is a sculptor or an artist and they actually carved it themselves?"

Rav put up his eyebrows. "I hadn't thought of that." He pushed his chair back and walked over to the whiteboards where the crime scene photos were taped up. "Come on, we'll have a look."

Kate and Rav perused the photographs of the statue. Rav looked so closely his nose almost touched the paper. "It *could* be," was his final conclusion. Kate peered again and nodded.

"I agree. It's well done but it could be hand made." She looked at Rav as a further thought occurred to her. "What if the killer made it?"

Rav's eyebrows shot up again. "Yeah," he said, slowly. "But...I'm not sure how much further that's going to get us."

"Search for sculptors, stonework artists, something like that?" Kate suggested.

"Yeah. Okay. That's a possibility."

Kate gave him a thumb up. "You can have that one for free."

Rav grinned. Kate skipped back to her desk and reached for the telephone.

She spoke at some length with a DI Warner, who was chatty and warm, even if the resulting conversation didn't exactly help her.

"Oh yeah, it was a bloody balls-up from start to finish," DI Warner said. "Before my time here, of course," he added, somewhat hastily to Kate's mind. "But I'm not sure that you can consider Linda Scott a viable suspect. Those threats were made directly after the court case, when Greeling had just walked free. Emotions were running high on all sides."

"Right," Kate said, cursing silently in her mind. "So, she was never charged with anything?"

"No. No point. The poor woman had just lost her grand-daughter."

"I hear she tried to sue the force?"

"No. Again, she threatened to. But it was never going to happen. She had no money, for a start." DI Warner sighed. "There was a serious case review, lessons learned, you know the sort of thing."

"Yes, I know," said Kate. She asked DI Warner a few more questions but it was becoming clear that this was something of a dead end, so eventually, she thanked him for his time and said goodbye.

Kate leant back in her chair, tapping her pen against her chin. What now? She felt that familiar sense of frustration, of blockage, when a case seemed to be stuck immovably with no clear sense of how to proceed. She sighed and got up to make herself and Chloe a coffee.

Was it worth trying to head up to Whitehaven? Apart from the statue, it appeared to be the only link between the two victims, and it was a tenuous one at that. Kate handed Chloe her mug and sat back down again, irritably tapping her foot against the bottom bar of her desk.

A memory of Theo's suggestion came back to her and she shook her head in annoyance at herself at having forgotten. Kate turned to her computer again.

"Chloe, who's covering looking for similar cases, you know, other statues found?"

Chloe looked startled. "Don't know, bird. Don't think anyone's even got onto that yet – too many other things to do."

"Okay. Thanks." Kate scribbled on her to-do list, just in case that idea faded from memory entirely. *Look at murders in Whitehaven area around time of Amanda Cahillan being there.* As she looked up, she caught sight of Olbeck's empty office and sighed. She missed him. I'll call him later on, she promised herself. She also wondered about his empty office. Now she was a DI... was it worth proposing to DCI Weaver that she take over his office, just while he was on leave? Did she actually want to, though? She looked over at Chloe, her funny, attractive friend, and over at Rav. She would miss the banter, that was inescapable. Oh well. Kate parked the thought for another day and turned back to her computer, ready to begin the hunt.

***

THAT EVENING, ON LEAVING WORK, Kate remembered she'd promised herself to call Olbeck. Instead, she texted him, asking if she could pop around. When his text pinged back *sure, come for dinner*, she drove to the supermarket, mindful of her earlier mistake in bringing chocolate for the children. Instead, she perused the aisle of baby food and nappies, looking for something healthy and suitable for a nine month old. She settled on some organic biscuits in the shape of friendly animals, and an educational toy for Harry. Then she chose a decent bottle of wine and some olives for the grown ups.

This time, Olbeck and Jeff's house was much quieter than the last time she'd been there. Kate realised that that was because it was now past eight o'clock and both children were in bed. Jeff opened the door, wearing an apron and holding a dripping wooden spoon.

"Hello, darling. Mark said you'd be round."

Kate kissed his cheek and handed over the bag of gifts. "Sorry, it's late notice I know, but I never seem to see you these days."

"Yes, I know. Sorry I couldn't make the party, but you know, we don't want to leave the kids with babysitters yet—"

"It's fine, don't be daft."

"Mark's just putting Harry to bed. Come through and have a drink."

The kitchen and living room weren't in quite the

chaos that they had been on Kate's last visit. There was a plastic bucket of toys over by the fireplace and a muslin cloth dropped on the carpet but, other than that, the room looked normal – and inviting to Kate, tired as she was. She dropped onto the sofa with a sigh and stretched her legs out.

Jeff came in with a glass of red wine for her. "You're looking well, Kate."

"Thanks." She smiled at him as she took her drink. Jeff was looking tired but happy himself; dark circles under his eyes but a relaxed look to his face. "How's it going?"

They talked about the children for several minutes until Olbeck's footsteps could be heard in the hallway. He came in and walked straight up to Kate to give her a hug.

"Hey. So glad you came over."

Released, Kate made her own appraisal of him. He was unshaven and dressed in tracksuit bottoms and a hoody, but, like Jeff, looked both relaxed and exhausted.

"Harry wants you," he said to Jeff, who groaned and wheeled around to leave the room.

Olbeck sat down next to Kate. "So, how's it going at work?"

It was Kate's turn to groan. "Frustrating. Don't seem to be getting anywhere with anything."

"God, I remember *those* days."

"Do you miss work?" Kate, having remembered

Anderton's wistful remark after the party, wanted to know.

"Yes. I actually do." Olbeck ran a hand over his stubbled jaw. "Being a parent is *tiring*. Now I understand it when people say they go to work for a rest."

"But it's okay, though?" Kate asked, suddenly anxious. "I mean, it's going okay?"

Olbeck smiled. "Yes, it's fine. It's a real challenge though, I won't lie."

"And you and Jeff... You're okay?"

"Sure. We don't have five minutes to spend together anymore, but I suppose that's normal when you've got two under five."

"It probably is." Kate got up and gave him a hug. "You're doing brilliantly. I'm proud of you."

Chapter Sixteen

"THANKS FOR DINNER," KATE SAID, getting up from her dining table and taking her plate to the dishwasher. "I must say, I'm getting spoiled with all this home cooking."

"Well, I've got the time now." Anderton pushed his chair back and stood up. "I like the fact that you appreciate it, though."

"I do." Kate gave him a grateful kiss. "Now, I really have to go through these files."

"Are these the murder cases in Whitehaven?"

"Yes, or close to it."

Anderton pulled up a chair and sat down next to Kate. "Let me help."

Kate pushed over the folders. "Be my guest." She reached for the top file and opened it. Merlin jumped up into her lap and curled up like a black, furry comma. She watched Anderton studying the files, his hand absentmindedly churning his hair as was his habit.

On impulse, she said "Can I put my cards on the table?"

Anderton looked up and smiled. "Yes. Okay, yes. I agree. We should move in together."

Kate felt her mouth drop open. "*What*?"

"Oh, that wasn't what you were going to ask?"

"No, it wasn't!"

"Oh." Anderton smiled again. "Well, I still think that it might be worth talking about at some point."

Kate blew out her cheeks. "Yes, you're probably right. Wow."

"I've been thinking about it for a while. But you've been so busy, it just never really seemed to be the right time to mention it."

"Okay, I have thought about it too," admitted Kate. "But I didn't mention it, because I wasn't sure it was what you wanted." She made a giant effort to gather her thoughts back on track. "Anyway, let's have that conversation another time. But soon."

"Okay. What were you going to say?"

Kate leant forward and took his hand. "What do you think about going back to work?"

She felt his hand tighten in hers. There was a short silence.

"Ah." Anderton withdrew his hand and sat back. "That was unexpected."

Kate felt her stomach tighten at his tone, but she pressed on. "It's just...I saw you at the party. With everyone. You even *said* it was good for us all to be back together again."

Anderton sighed. "If it was that easy, Kate..."

"I know it's not that easy." Kate swallowed, thought better and then thought again. "I know you...you've perhaps lost confidence. I don't see how you could not have done—"

"I haven't lost confidence." Anderton sounded angry, and Kate felt her heart sink. She should not have brought this up.

"Okay. All right. Maybe I shouldn't have said anything."

"No. Maybe you shouldn't have."

They regarded each other with solemn faces. Then Anderton appeared to shake himself.

"Perhaps I'll stay at mine tonight."

"Oh, don't be like that—"

"I'm tired, Kate."

On the verge of saying something provocative, Kate folded her lips together. *I'm learning.* She took a deep, deep breath. "Okay. Perhaps you should."

Anderton looked faintly surprised, as if he'd been expecting her to argue with him. Kate forced herself to smile at him. "We're all tired, *Selwyn.*"

She scarcely ever used Anderton's first name. Nor did anyone else. For most of the officers at the station, Anderton *was* their former DCI's given name. It had taken Kate weeks once they were romantically attached to actually ask for his Christian name, and even now, she tended not to use it, mostly because it made him wince every time she did.

"Oh," said Anderton. "Like that, is it?"

"What do you mean?"

"You only ever call me Selwyn when you're extremely pissed off with me."

It was Kate's turn to sigh. I'm too old and too tired for all this drama, she told herself. "Seriously, why don't you go home? I'm knackered, and I've got all this work to get through."

***

THEY KISSED GOODBYE AT THE door, but it was perfunctory. Kate watched him drive away with a coiled knot of anxiety in her stomach. They had had fights before, of course they had, but this felt...different. Was it because something had fundamentally changed between them? Or was it because Kate had refused to rise to the bait, for once?

Kate shut the front door and locked it, conscious of a rising dark mood. She stomped into the kitchen and poured the last of the red wine from the bottle into her glass. Merlin coiled like smoke around her ankles.

"Bloody *men*," said Kate, to him. She sat back down at the table and spread the case files out so she could look at them properly. Was this really the right time to do this? She was exhausted, emotional and she'd had two—she took a large gulp—nearly *three* glasses of wine. Her bed appealed. But there was something else tugging at her, something she'd had since she first walked through the doors of the Abbeyford station all those years ago. She wanted to solve this case. The victims always deserved justice.

Something else occurred to her and her fingers tightened on the stem of the wine glass. If these two cases were connected, if the killer in both cases was the same, then what if there were going to be more?

Kate took another large gulp and bent her head to the table, trying to focus. Her argument with Anderton was almost forgotten.

Chapter Seventeen

KATE WAS THE FIRST IN the office the next morning, despite a bad night's sleep. So eager was she to show the others what she'd discovered, she'd bounded out of bed before her alarm even went off, dressing herself warmly as she could see the frost glittering on the ground outside when she drew her bedroom curtains back.

Rav was the first one to arrive after her, and Kate hurried across to his desk as he divested himself of scarf, gloves and hat.

"*God*, it's cold."

"I know." Kate couldn't care less about discussing the weather. "Guess what I've found?"

Rav grinned. "It's obviously something good. Can I have coffee first?"

"If you must." Kate waited impatiently while he made them both a cup. As Rav carried the steaming mugs back to his desk, Chloe came into the office.

"What's up, bird?"

"Found something." Kate withdrew the relevant

copy of the photograph from her plastic folder. "Take a gander at *this*."

Both Rav and Chloe regarded the paper that Kate proffered. Sharp-eyed Rav was the first to spot it.

"Bloody hell." His forefinger shot out to land on the photograph. Chloe gasped.

"It's the statue. Shit."

Kate took a moment to bask in the heady glow of a job well done. "Yes. The same statue."

Chloe grabbed the paper off her as if she was afraid it would disappear. "What's the case? The vic? Who is it?"

Kate handed her the file. "It's in here. The victim was a sixty year old man, found in his home with multiple stab wounds. Rather like Roland Barry."

Chloe was rapidly reading the file papers. "His name was William Bathford. Retired care home owner." She looked up straight into Kate's eyes. "What kind of care home? Elderly? Or children?"

"All I've got is in there," said Kate, waving at the folder in Chloe's hands. "I need to liaise with the Whitehaven station to get the nitty-gritty."

By now, Theo had entered the office. "What's up, guys?"

They filled him in. Theo raised his dark eyebrows. "Okay. Okay. Nice work. Anyone told Nicola yet?"

"I'll do that," Kate said, smartly. "In fact, I'll go and do it now." She tipped him a wink. "Don't worry, I'll tell her it was your idea."

DCI Weaver preferred people to make official appointments to see her through her PA, but Kate thought that a breakthrough of this magnitude surely warranted an impromptu visit. She knocked at her door, clutching the file on William Bathford, praying, surely for the first time in her life, that Nicola was in.

Since the party, Kate had been conscious of a slight thawing of DCI Weaver's usual attitude towards her. Whether that was because Kate had herself begun to behave in a more friendly, mature manner towards her boss was something Kate, rather uncomfortably, had considered. Or perhaps Nicola was just tiring of being such a constant bitch. Whichever the reason, Kate was thankful.

She told DCI Weaver what she had discovered and was rewarded by the sight of a genuine smile spreading across Nicola's face.

"That's fantastic. Well done, Kate."

Ooh, I got a 'Kate'. Not a 'DS, I mean DI Redman'. Things are looking up. Kate said nothing but smiled back in return.

"This is very promising. Same MO. Same figure at the crime scene." DCI Weaver bit her lip as she read through the file. "God, we could be looking at a serial killer, here."

"What do you want me to do?" asked Kate.

"Stop whatever it is you were doing on the Callihan case and throw yourself at this one. I'm sending you up to Whitehaven so you can interview the people who worked on this case."

Kate clenched her fist in triumph under the cover

of the table. Since DCI Weaver had taken over, Kate had been the only one kept office-bound in far-flung investigations. *God bless that Halloween party—or whatever it is that's making her nicer to me.* "Fantastic," she said, out loud. "I'll go up tomorrow."

The rest of the morning passed in a blur of organisation: care for Merlin, booking a budget hotel up in Whitehaven, arranging the handover of Kate's current cases to the others in the team. It was sometimes possible for two officers to travel up together to interview witnesses but not this time. "You're on your own," DCI Weaver had stated. "We're too busy to spare more than one of you at the moment." Kate didn't mind. What with working all day surrounded by other people and now, with Anderton, not getting much space at home, she was almost relishing the thought of some time to herself.

As she had that thought, she remembered the words she and Anderton had exchanged the night before. She felt the smile fall from her face. She hadn't heard from him since; not that she'd contacted him, either, but that was more to do with how busy she'd been rather than making a point. Should she send him a text, tell him that she was going to be away for a few days? Her fingers hovered over the screen of her phone. Then she shook her head and put the mobile away. Not that she wanted to be petty, but...

She got home later than normal that night, having spent the afternoon setting up various interviews with the officers and the witnesses of the Bathford case. Merlin twined around her ankles as she shut the front door behind her and locked it securely. Kate slung the chicken risotto that she'd picked up in the supermarket in the microwave and flicked on the switch of the kettle. She'd once almost lived on ready meals and pre-prepared salads but, since she'd been seeing Anderton, she'd been fed with a lovingly home-cooked meal several times a week. Kate regarded the spinning package as it rotated in the microwave, feeling depressed. Really, they'd only had a row. Not the first, either. He'll be back, she told herself. And if he isn't...

Frowning, she opened the refrigerator and took out a bottle of wine. Was this really a relationship that was ever going to work? The age difference, the fact he'd been married before, her relationship with his children (which was cordial but distant). Did she want children? That was normally a thought she shied away from, packed away down deep, but now she tried to face it, taking a gulp of wine.

When Kate was seventeen, she'd had a baby. The baby had been adopted, and it was only through a lot of time, therapy and introspection that Kate could reconcile herself with her decision. She was more at peace with what she had done now than she ever had been before, but she was horribly afraid that if she had another child, all those painful memories would come flooding back. Could she go through that again?

It had taken so much effort to move past the pain. Kate found herself shutting her eyes, warding off the thought.

That was even supposing Anderton—if he hadn't dumped her already—*wanted* more children. A man in his fifties, with grown-up children, would probably not want to go back to the newborn baby stage; late nights, nappies, bottles. It was something they had never talked about. Kate sat down on her sofa, feeling thoroughly miserable. After a moment, she reached for her mobile and tapped out a message to Anderton. *I'm off up North to Whitehaven tomorrow so driving most of the day. Talk to you in the evening if you're free. X.*

It felt rather more stiff and formal than she would have liked. To hell with it. Kate picked at her microwave meal, finished off the wine and headed up to bed. Perhaps tomorrow would be a better day.

Chapter Eighteen

KATE HIT THE ROAD BRIGHT and early the next morning, cheered by a reasonable night's sleep and the prospect of a sunny day. The prevailing day's brisk wind had mostly stripped the trees of their leaves and their branches were outlined sharply against a blue sky. Kate fortified herself for the journey with various CDs, snacks and a flask of coffee. Then she gave Merlin a goodbye stroke, told him Janet would be in to feed him later, and let herself out of the house.

She was so early that there was little traffic on the roads, and she was able to get out of Abbeyford reasonably quickly. She'd considered taking the train—Kate's favourite method of transport—but knew that if she had lots of people to interview, having a car would be a distinct advantage. As she joined the M4, she heard the ping of a text message coming through on her phone and it took every ounce of will power she possessed not to pull over on the hard shoulder and see if it was from Anderton.

She stopped for fuel after half an hour and grabbed her mobile. Anderton had written that he'd talk to her later. So, at least he was still talking to her. Smiling, Kate paid for her petrol and set off again, feeling better.

She got to Whitehaven just as dusk was falling. The beauty of the Lake District would have to wait for the morning. Kate found her hotel without any drama and checked in. She was hungry and decided to have a decent dinner before beginning her interview preparations for tomorrow.

Chloe rang just as she was lifting the final forkful of steak to her mouth.

"Hey, bird, how's it going up there?"

"I haven't seen anyone yet. It took me almost all day to drive up here."

"That's what I thought. Hey, I can't talk for long."

"Got a hot date with Roman?" Kate teased, intending it as a joke, but Chloe replied in the affirmative, rather smugly. "Oh. Great. Well, have fun."

"Who are you seeing tomorrow?"

"DI Randall. He was the investigating officer on the Bathford case. Hopefully he'll be able to give me the run down and I can start to see if anything gels with our cases."

"Mm." Chloe sounded distracted and Kate could hear rustling noises in the background.

"Look, I'll call you tomorrow. Enjoy your date."

They said goodbye and Kate, yawning, ordered another glass of red wine. She knew she should be going through the few case notes she had before her meeting tomorrow, but the thought was not tempting. She checked her phone again to see if she'd missed a call from Anderton. Should she call him? Kate was not fond of public telephone conversations. Wearily, she opened her briefcase and extracted the notes she'd already made.

Two years ago, William Bathford's body had been discovered at his home by his son. He had lived alone since his divorce, five years previously, and had retired from his job the year before his death. Kate rapidly read over her notes. Just as in the Barry case, there was no sign of forced entry, no sign of a struggle. The body had suffered multiple stab wounds. Kate looked once more at the crime scene photograph of the living room and that mysterious statue, wings spread, the blank oval of the woman's face looking out over the carnage. *Erinyes*. The Furies. Kate bit her lip, regarding the photograph and thinking. Then she read through the Wikipedia page on the subject, which she'd printed out before her journey. It was the second or third time she'd read it. "Deities of vengeance," she murmured under her breath. That was the phrase that kept leaping out at her. Vengeance. But for what? And was she right?

She recalled DCI Weaver's words to her the day before, her mention of a possible serial killer being on the loose. Kate remembered the case she'd worked a few years ago now, where the bodies of young men began to appear in graveyards, white and still. Serial killings were still rare in the United Kingdom. Was it likely that this could be another? Kate couldn't quite recall the standard definition, but three killings in under three years surely would qualify? If it *was* the same killer. "If, if, if," she said to herself quietly. Then she drained her glass of the final mouthful of wine, packed her papers away, and went back to her room.

Anderton rang just as she was getting into her pyjamas. Kate answered the call with a twinge of anxiety in the pit of her stomach. "Hello."

"How was the drive up?" Anderton sounded normal. Kate felt herself relax.

"Long and tiring."

"I'll bet. What are you doing now?"

Kate yawned. "Sorry. I should be reading over my notes but they're blurring in front of my eyes, quite frankly."

"Hm. I remember those days." Anderton hesitated and then went on, a shade more diffidently. "Listen, Kate, I'm sorry for the other day. You took me by surprise, that's all."

"So did *you*." Kate struggled to get the covers of the bed untucked from beneath the mattress. "God, why do they always make these beds so tightly?" Eventually, she freed the sheets enough to enable her to slip beneath them. "Anyway, do you want to talk about it now?"

"Not really. But I think we need to have a discussion on a few things when you get back, don't you?"

Kate felt that twinge of anxiety again. "Yes. I suppose so." She yawned again, unable to help it.

"Look, get some sleep. Are you coming back tomorrow?"

"The day after."

"Then that's when I'll see you."

"Night, then."

She listened to the two-tone beep that terminated the call and then rolled over and put her mobile on the bedside table. She lay back amongst the many pillows, slightly comforted by the fact that she and Anderton seemed to have smoothed things out, if only a little. Kate closed her eyes. *Say what you like about budget hotels, but by God, their beds are comfortable.* She was asleep in moments.

DI Randall turned out to be a cheerful looking man with a head of hair that shaded from bright ginger to a sandy gold and rather attractive blue eyes. He greeted Kate affably and led her through to an interview room at the Whitehaven police station.

"You've no doubt done some background research on the case," he told Kate as they sat down at the interview table. "But I'm sure I'll be able to flesh it out a bit more. Tell me again what the connection is?"

Kate produced her evidence; notes and photographs of the identical statue found. DI Randall took the photograph of the Barry murder scene, where Kate had ringed the location of the statue in red pen.

"Uncanny," he said, glancing at her with those blue eyes. "It's identical, isn't it?"

"Indeed. So, you can see why we're interested in spotting any other connections between the cases. It's not just the murder of Roland Barry, either. We very recently had a second murder in Abbeyford, that of a young—fairly young—woman called Amanda Callihan." Kate handed him her notes on the Callihan case and let him read them. Once he'd looked over them, he nodded for her to continue and she did so. "There's another link we've established between your case and Amanda's. She used to work here, as a social worker."

DI Randall nodded again. "Social worker? Well, William Bathford ran a children's care home. Perhaps Amanda—what was her last name again?"

"Callihan."

"Right. Perhaps Amanda Callihan had contact with him or with the home in a professional capacity."

Kate leant forward. "Yes, that's something I'll be looking into with the council while I'm up here. It was a few years ago but they might be able to help."

"Yes." DI Randall regarded the photographs again and perused Kate's notes once more. "It's weird though..."

"What is?"

He put his finger on the circled statues in each crime scene picture one after another. "This. This...

calling card, I suppose you'd could call it. Have you tracked down the manufacturer yet?"

Kate shook her head. "We're working on the possibility that they might be handmade or produced overseas."

"Okay." Another flash of blue as he met her eyes. "Has anyone broached the possibility that you're looking at a serial killer yet?"

It was Kate's turn to use her eyes; she cast them up. "Of course that's been flagged."

"That's what's weird. Have you ever worked a serial case before?"

Kate felt an impulse in her arm to reach around to the small of her back, to press against the small raised semi-circle of scar tissue left there by a killer's knife. She repressed it. "Yes. Two of them."

DI Randall raised his eyebrows, making an impressed face. "Right. So, you know how unusual it is for them to kill across gender, sex, whatever you want to call it."

Kate knew. "It must happen, though. But I agree, it's incredibly rare. Like killing across ethnicities."

"Yeah, exactly. And these MOs... The woman, Amanda—that's just totally different. What was it, a blow to the head?" He consulted Kate's notes again. "Oh, right. Strangulation but before that, she was laid out by a blow to the head. And then you've got the men, Bathford and Barry. Viciously stabbed to death. That's a hell of a change. I mean, I could understand it better if Amanda had been the *first* victim. You get the serials who start escalating; time between killings, killings get more vicious, sadistic because they're chasing the high—" He caught Kate's expression and cleared his throat. "Anyway, you know what I mean. But to have two really violent stabbings and *then* a strangulation... Well, as you know, DI Redman, that is odd..."

They looked at each other in silence. Eventually Kate nodded. "I know. It's been bothering me too."

DI Randall looked down again at the notes. "Could it be that the statue is actually a coincidence?" He murmured the question, almost to himself. "That Amanda's death isn't actually connected?"

"I know," repeated Kate. "But *what* a coincidence. The exact same statue at all three scenes, none of which the victims appear to have bought for themselves."

"Hmm." DI Randall put down the paper and blew out his cheeks. "Got any forensic links between the cases?"

"We're working on it. You know how it is, there's always a constant backlog for them to process."

"I know it. Well, I'll tell you what. I'll pull everything we've got on the Bathford case for you and you can wade through it to your heart's content. Have you got anything else planned?"

"The trip to the council, to talk to Amanda Callihan's previous employers," Kate reminded him.

"Oh, right. Do you know how to get to the council offices?"

"I've got sat nav." Kate smiled at him, prompting a smile back.

"Right. Have you been to Whitehaven before?"

"No. I've never been this far north. I'm hoping to see a bit of the Lakes when I head home."

"Yes, don't miss that." DI Randall hesitated for a second and then said, rather diffidently, "I don't know if you've got dinner plans or anything for tonight but if not, I could show you a nice restaurant. If you want to, that is."

Kate was silent for a moment. Was he asking her out of friendliness or, well, something more? Anderton's face popped into her mind. "Um...I'm not sure yet," was what she came out with, smiling to take any sting away. "Let me see how I get on with the paperwork today and I'll let you know, if that's okay?"

"Oh, sure, sure, sure, no problem." DI Randall was laughing, slightly too uneasily. "No problem, DI Redman. It was just an idea."

"Please, call me Kate," Kate said, taking pity on him.

"Right. Kate. Well, I'll let you get on."

The door shut behind him, and Kate permitted herself a quiet giggle. For some reason, she found herself thinking of Chloe. How *did* people date these days? She thought of Anderton again, but this time with a rush of love. She pulled out her mobile and texted him on impulse. *Missing you xxx.* Then she squared her shoulders, took a deep breath and set to work.

Chapter Nineteen

LATE THAT SAME AFTERNOON, KATE went looking for DI Randall, cardboard folder in her hand. She found his office and knocked on the door.

"Any luck?" he asked her. He looked relaxed again and Kate realised that she did actually find him quite attractive. *Hmm, perhaps dinner isn't such a good idea, Kate.*

"I did, actually. It may be nothing, but – well, I just wondered if I could run it past you?"

"Of course. Come in."

Kate shut the door behind her and sat down opposite him. "I went through everything remotely connected with William Bathford. Apparently, one of the girls from the home, a Karen Black, came to this station in the late nineteen nineties, and reported that she'd been sexually abused by him. She apparently had made another accusation about him before but I can't find any record of that at all."

DI Randall lifted his eyebrows. "Right. So there was an investigation?"

Kate pulled a face. "Actually, I'm not sure there was.

Apparently, this girl, Karen, had a history of reporting abuse. She grew up in care and she reported several of her foster families. I think they were investigated and nothing was found."

DI Randall leant forward. "So, she reported it and nothing was done?"

Kate flipped through the pages of a report. "Nothing was done. Until another girl, a Melanie Smith, reported Bathford as well."

"Ah. Can I have a look?" Kate handed over the folder and DI Randall began to read.

Kate let him read for a minute and then spoke again. "Anyway, there was an investigation into the home, but after a few weeks, Melanie Smith withdrew her accusation. She said Karen had bullied her into reporting it and it wasn't true. So, any case against Bathford collapsed, and the investigation was stopped."

DI Randall looked up from the file. "Right. So, what happened then? Sorry, I know I'm the one who works here, but this was way before my time. I was in London then." They both laughed before he carried on. "What happened to the girls?"

Kate grimaced. "Melanie Smith was placed in another care home. Karen ran away. I haven't been able to trace her yet."

"Oh dear."

"Exactly. Anyway, when I go to the council tomorrow, I'm going to see if I can find a link to what happened with these girls and whether Amanda Callihan was involved in any way."

DI Randall looked impressed. "That sounds like a good plan."

"Thank you." Kate sat back in her chair and folded her hands in her lap. On impulse, she said "If that dinner invitation's still available, I'll take you up on it."

DI Randall looked both surprised and pleased. "Oh, yeah, sure. When are you ready to go?"

"Whenever you are." Just for safety's sake, Kate added, "I just need to get back to my hotel at a reasonable hour. I've got to give my partner a call."

"Sure."

***

THE RESTAURANT THAT HE TOOK her to was within walking distance of the Whitehaven station, and on the way, Kate was able to take in a bit more of the city. It was prettily situated around a curving harbour, but Kate could see that it was far from a wealthy area. The streets were lined with betting shops, pound shops and charity shops. The restaurant was a pleasant surprise though; a family-run Italian place, with a black and white tiled floor and pictures of the Italian coast on the walls.

"Have you lived here long?" Kate asked when they were seated.

"About five years now. I moved up from London."

DI Randall handed her a menu and sat back in his chair. "My ex-wife had family around here, so we thought it would be a good idea to move closer."

Kate felt rather awkward. Was he signalling to her that he was single? "Right," was what she said, in a tone she hoped would shut down any further information on DI Randall's romantic history. "What's your first name, by the way?"

DI Randall smiled. "It's Tom."

"Tom, can you tell me what *you* think about the Bathford murder? What are your theories on it?"

Tom Randall took a sip from his glass of wine. "Well..."

Kate persisted. "Whatever you think. What have you got?"

"Well," he repeated. Then he leaned forward. "The thing is, what you said about this—this Karen. She's pegged as a liar because she's reported people for things that they don't seem to have done. Clearly, she's troubled; she's a troubled young woman. Troubled young *child*. She's probably been sexually abused in the past, not by the people she's accusing but by someone else, someone else who's got away with it."

Kate was listening intently. "Go on."

"Well, say her accusation against Bathford—and I'm purely speculating here—say she was telling the truth?"

Kate stared at him. "So Bathford was guilty of sexually abusing her and the other girl, Melanie."

"It's purely a theory but I've been thinking about it on the walk over here. Just because someone's made false accusations in the past doesn't necessarily mean that they're lying about what genuinely happened to them at a later stage."

"True." Kate was interrupted in her sentence by the arrival of their main courses. She sat back, allowing the waitress to position the plates and offer black pepper to them both. Once the woman had left, she leant forward again. "So, say we take it as read that Karen and Melanie are telling the truth. Bathford *had* sexually abused them."

"Yes."

Kate picked up her fork and began twisting spaghetti around it. "So, if you were one of the victims, how would not being believed make you feel?"

"Bloody angry, I'd expect."

"Exactly."

They ate for a few minutes before Kate wiped her mouth with the napkin and spoke again. "But the trouble with that theory is, as I'm sure you'll agree, Bathford wasn't killed at the time of the accusations. It was later. *Years* later."

"I know."

Kate bent her head to her plate. "So, it could have absolutely nothing to do with this, whatsoever."

"It's a possibility," agreed Tom.

Kate sighed. She pushed a few more mouthfuls of spaghetti in and chewed thoughtfully.

"Well," said Tom. "One thing we could do is try and track down these two girls. Karen and Melanie. Find out what they're up to now."

"Yes. That would be a given."

"I can do that tomorrow." Tom reached for the wine bottle and topped up Kate's glass. "No problem."

"Thank you. I've got the council visit tomorrow so hopefully I'll be able to prove a link between Amanda Cahill and the children's home."

"Good luck."

They talked about other things for the remainder of the meal. Kate found him an easy conversationalist. From time to time she was conscious of that flash of attraction she'd felt in his office and batted the thought away. She stuck to two glasses of wine as well. She'd mentioned Anderton as her partner, but as the evening wore on, she was conscious that Tom might, just *might*, have interpreted that as Kate having a police partner, not a romantic one. Try as she might, she couldn't think of a way of bringing the subject up without looking odd or, as was actually the case, as if she suspected Tom on having designs on her.

"Do you fancy having a drink somewhere?" asked Tom as he paid the bill. Kate had offered her fair share, but he'd waved her away.

"Sorry, I can't." She decided to be brutally honest. "I have to give my boyfriend a call."

"Oh." Although he hid it well, there was a moment

when Tom looked completely crestfallen. "Oh, well, never mind."

Kate took pity on him. "I've had a lovely evening, thank you. And thanks for offering to track down those girls for me."

"My pleasure." The fact that Tom reacted so graciously made Kate like him all the more. *Anderton*, she reminded herself.

"See you tomorrow, then." She held out her hand to be shaken.

"Good night."

Kate gave him a farewell smile and left the restaurant. Walking back to her hotel, she blew out her cheeks. *When does life get any easier?* She shook off the thought and pulled her coat tighter about her neck, warding off the chill northern breeze.

Chapter Twenty

THE COUNCIL OFFICER THAT KATE met with the next morning was a lady who looked as if she was fast approaching retirement. In fact, as she mentioned in passing, Lucy Masterfield was only in her fifties but the stress and worry of her job had aged her beyond her years. She had grey hair cut brutally short, stooped shoulders and, in a contrast that was oddly touching, earrings that were shaped like strawberries.

"Pleased to meet you, DI Redman. I hope I can be of assistance. I *have* been here a long time."

"Thank you, Mrs Masterfield."

"Oh, do call me Lucy."

Kate smiled at her. "Right. Thanks, Lucy. I'm trying to find out as much as I can about one of your former social workers. Amanda Callihan. She worked in Whitehaven from nineteen ninety six to the early noughties, I think, when she resigned from the job."

Lucy Masterfield took the file that Kate held out to her. She wore no rings on her hands and her nails were short and unpolished. "Yes, I remember her. She was a nice girl. And you say she's been murdered?" Her face puckered for a moment. "That's awful."

"Yes. I'm sorry." Kate waited for a moment and then spoke again. "That's why we're trying to find out as much as we can about her work up here, as we think it might have a bearing on her case."

Lucy Masterfield nodded. "Right, I understand."

Kate went on. "I'm particularly keen on finding out if she had any link with a particular children's care home, the Carndale. Could I have that folder for a second?" She took it back from Lucy and extracted a photograph. "This is the place."

Lucy took the photograph. "Yes. Yes, I remember this. It's closed now. In fact, wasn't there something... The chap running it was killed, wasn't he?"

"Yes, he was. We're thinking that there's a link between the two cases."

Lucy's eyebrows lifted. "And you think Amanda might be that link?"

"Did she have any dealings with the place?"

"I can soon find out." Lucy beckoned Kate over and pointed to the kettle, over on the counter by the wall. "Help yourself to a coffee and I'll dig down into the archives and see what I can find."

Kate did as she suggested, making one for Lucy as well. She waited, leaning against the counter, and watched Lucy tapping away at her computer. Lucy, as if she felt Kate's gaze, turned around. "I'll be a while here. Did you want to find yourself somewhere more comfortable to sit?"

"Actually, I need to make a few calls. I'll be back in half an hour or so."

***

KATE NEGOTIATED HER WAY OUT of the unfamiliar building and stepped out into a fresh breeze, a faint hint of salt carried with it. Why *did* the sea smell so good? She took in a few, deep inhalations and turned her attention to her phone.

Anderton, first. Kate genuinely had tried to call him on her return from the restaurant last night, but the call had gone straight to voicemail. She left him a light hearted message and then tried the office. Theo answered.

"All right, mate? How are they treating you up north?"

Kate filled him in on her discovery. "We're still waiting to see if there is an evidential link between Amanda Cahill and the Carndale children's home."

"You want to talk to the boss?"

Kate didn't, particularly. "No point, Theo. Let me wait until I've actually got something—or not. Has anything else come up your end?"

She heard Theo's irritated sigh in her ear. "Not a lot, mate. Rav's still not been able to track down the manufacturer of those statues. We've had forensics back though, so I'm going through them."

"Ok. Listen, can you do me a favour. If you're too busy with that, Chloe could do it. Can you run a check on these two names: Melanie Smith and Karen Black." Kate spelled them out for him and added, "Just see if anything comes up." She knew that DI Randall was doing a similar search but Theo was good at tracking people down, and more eyes on the job couldn't hurt. "Thanks, Theo. I'll check in later and I'm back tomorrow, pending anything explosive up here."

"Laters, mate."

As Kate hung up, she pondered whether a DI should actually be allowing a DS to call them 'mate'. But then, what was the harm? She could just see the look on Theo's face if she requested he address her more formally. Grinning, she wondered whether it was worth doing, just for a laugh. Then her phone rang—Anderton, finally calling her back—and she dismissed the thought.

When Kate got back to Lucy Masterfield's desk (she had only taken one wrong turn and was soon back on track), Lucy had a small pile of computer print-outs by the side of her keyboard. Kate's stomach twisted in anticipation.

She sat down opposite Lucy, trying not to look too eager. "Did you manage to get anything?"

Lucy smiled. "Yes, I did. Amanda Callihan wrote several reports on the Carndale children's home. She was the social worker for several of the children there." She handed Kate the pile of printed paper. "I'm sure you'll be able to see what I mean."

Kate clutched the paper in one hand. "Was she the council liaison for Karen Black or Melanie Smith?"

"For both. She had several meetings with both."

Under the table, Kate clenched her free hand in

triumph. "That's great, Lucy, thank you so much. That's just what I needed."

Lucy smiled again and it illuminated her tired, wrinkled face into something like beauty. "That's good. I'm glad I could help."

"I'm going to take these and read them through." Kate stood up and extended her hand. Lucy shook it. "And for what it's worth, I'd like to thank you."

"Thank me?"

"Yes. I sometimes think I have a difficult job but then I meet you guys, and I realise I actually have it easy. So, thank you."

Again, that illuminating smile. "Thank *you*, DI Redman."

***

KATE DROVE BACK TO THE Whitehaven police station, her stomach fluttering with anticipation. This was it; she could feel it. Veteran of many an investigation, she knew that in almost every one, you hit paydirt. You found the lead, the suspect, the motive. A small part of each, perhaps, but something you could work with.

She bounded up the steps of the station and hurried for DI Randall's office, sure of her way there now. He wasn't there, and Kate clicked her tongue with annoyance. Then, deciding on something, she picked up his desk phone and dialled her own desk number.

Chloe answered the phone. "Hey, bird. How's it going up there?"

"It's going great. I've found something." Kate gave Chloe a succinct run down of what she'd discovered.

"Fantastic." Kate could hear the smile in Chloe's voice. "So, what now?"

"Can you put me through to Nicola?" Kate thought that DCI Weaver, now treating her more fairly, deserved to be referred to in less formal (and indeed, less insulting) terms than she normally used.

"Hold on." There were rustles and beeps before Chloe came back on the line. "She's on a conference call."

"Don't worry, I'll email."

Just as Kate was saying goodbye, Tom Randall walked into his office. He looked surprised to see Kate sitting at his desk.

"Don't worry, I'm not after your job," Kate said with a grin. "Just wanted to use your phone."

"Be my guest." Tom placed a cardboard folder in front of her. "I've got something for you."

Kate looked at him eagerly. "You've found the two girls?"

"No, unfortunately. I have found one, though. Melanie Smith. It's all in here." Kate reached a hand for the folder. Tom added, rather plaintively, "Can I have my seat back now?"

"Sorry." Kate gathered her things together. "Here, have your desk back too. Thanks for this, Tom."

She found a spare desk and read through the new information. Melanie Smith had been born in 1983, which would have made her fifteen in 1998. Kate did a rapid head-calculation and worked out that Melanie would now be thirty-four. She didn't appear to have married, or if she had, she'd kept her name. Kate looked at the address and raised her eyebrows. Melanie was now living in Bristol, right on the doorstep of the Abbeyford force's jurisdiction.

Kate made up her mind. Melanie needed to be interviewed as a matter of urgency, and although she knew that Chloe, Rav, or Theo would be quite capable of doing so, Kate found herself strangely protective over her right to question the suspect. After all, she was the one who'd found the link between the crimes, hadn't she? She pushed aside the thought that, as a DI, she probably should be delegating a little more. *Sod it*. She stuffed the papers into her laptop case and went to find DI Randall, to say goodbye.

Chapter Twenty One

IT WAS ALMOST ELEVEN O'CLOCK at night by the time Kate made it back to Abbeyford. Tired as she was, she headed for the police station. She needed to type up her report for DCI Weaver, and that would be best done at her desk. If she went home and sat down, she'd fall asleep.

Wearily, she parked the car, locked it and trudged towards the back entrance. There was someone fronting the reception area at all times, but Kate was feeling too tired to have to make small talk. Yawning, she climbed the stairs, her hand trailing the plastic coating of the banister, her laptop case banging against her hip.

As she walked down the corridor, she noticed a light on in DCI Weaver room. Pulling a late one, thought Kate, with some admiration. All the better, as now she could give her a verbal report now and type it up formally in the morning. Kate knocked gently on the closed office door. Then she knocked again. Finally, she pushed it open.

"It's just me—" she began and pulled herself up

with a gasp. There, on her desk, was Nicola Weaver, semi-dressed and in a tangle of limbs with—*My god! Is it? Yes, it is!*–Theo.

For a frozen moment, the two of them stared in horror at Kate, who stood as if turned to marble. Then, coming to her senses, she gasped, "Sorry, sorry!" and pulled the door closed with a slam.

Oh God, oh God. Kate ran for the incident room with her hand to her mouth. *Oh, God!* Why had she opened that bloody door? *Why*? And how long had *that* been going on? She threw herself into her chair and put her head on the table, cringing. *Jesus.* She tried to unsee what she'd just witnessed but it was impossible. Kate groaned and considered her options. She should probably just go home. Oh, God, how was she going to face Nicola tomorrow? And Theo... Kate remembered the funny conversation they'd had some time ago, when she'd had the suspicion that he'd been talking about a girlfriend. Had he been referring to Nicola? *Oh, God...*

Belatedly, it occurred to Kate that she didn't have a judgemental leg to stand on. What had Anderton been when they'd first slept together? Yes, that's right—her immediate boss. DCI Weaver might have twenty years on Theo but how much older was Anderton than Kate? Kate blew out her cheeks and sat up, smoothing her hair back from her face. Okay, how to handle this?

Firstly, she was going to get the hell out of the office, and if that meant she had to escape through the front of the station, then that what was going to happen. The thought of having to pass Nicola's office again and run the risk of the two of them coming across her was a thought to make Kate wince. And tomorrow? Well, *clearly* the best thing to do was to be completely English about it all and pretend it had never happened.

She grabbed her bag and crept towards the office door, holding her breath to see if she could hear voices or footsteps. There was silence. Kate ran noiselessly towards the front stairs, holding her bag against her. Once she'd left the station and got to her car, the first giggle escaped her. *Oh, Lord, just imagine what Nicola and Theo are going through now...* As mortified as Kate was, she could only imagine what they must be feeling. Really, it would be a kindness not to mention anything... Laughing softly to herself, Kate put the car in gear and drove home.

She was still cringing for them the next morning as she ate her breakfast and prepared herself for the day ahead. Kate had half expected a text from Theo, pleading for silence or something similar, but radio silence held. Probably just as well, thought Kate. She picked Merlin up to give him an extra big snuggle, as penance for being away for the last couple of days.

She was so taken up with what had happened the night before that the developments in all three of the current cases had slipped her mind. The sight of a large black crow perched on top of her car reminded her. It eyed her balefully and flew away as she approached. Strange, thought Kate. Almost like an omen—but of what? She flung her coat and bag onto the passenger seat and started the engine. It was a lovely autumn day, blazing with golden sunshine, and despite the embarrassment Kate knew awaited her at work, she drove there in fairly cheerful spirits. These were further raised by Anderton texting her to ask her to dinner that night. Kate tapped out an affirmative answer when she got to the carpark of the station and, taking a deep breath— *Just pretend nothing happened, just pretend nothing happened*—she walked into the building.

She had to steel herself to walk past DCI Weaver's office, but the door was firmly shut. Blowing out her cheeks, Kate headed to her desk, realising with relief that Theo either wasn't in yet, or was out (or had resigned in sheer shame). Smiling to herself, Kate sat down and greeted Chloe. A small part of her— okay, quite a large part of her—wanted to share the gossip but, morally and ethically, she knew it would be a dreadful thing to do. Thankfully, she thought of Anderton, with whom she *would* share the news with.

"Welcome back, bird," Chloe said absently as she scrolled the wheel of her mouse. "So, a successful trip, yeah?"

"Yes. I've got a potential witness slash suspect to interview as a matter of urgency." Kate opened up the relevant database to run a background check on Melanie Smith. She printed off the relevant files and returned to her desk to peruse them more thoroughly. Melanie Smith had had a chequered youth. Convictions for shoplifting, for soliciting, drug convictions, once for assault. Kate pressed her lips together. Nothing too surprising for a child who'd been abandoned, who'd grown up in care, who—if the other girl, Karen Black, had been telling the truth— had been abused by the very people supposed to be protecting her. It was depressing, but it was expected. But did that mean that Melanie was capable of these much more serious and brutal crimes?

Kate decided not to phone ahead to announce her visit. Sometimes it was wise to interview people on the hop; they weren't able to prepare their stories quite so successfully if they were pre-warned. She collected her things and walked towards the door of the office where she managed to run almost slap bang into Theo, who was walking in.

"Sorry," gasped Kate, as she tried to regain her balance. Theo, naturally, apologised too. Kate's careful sense of what she'd been prepared to do when confronting him for the first time since it happened fell apart. She stuttered out something about hurrying off to an interview before realising that Theo was as equally embarrassed as she was. Possibly more.

Kate said a hurried goodbye and scurried off to the door of the office before slowing down. Taking a deep breath, she turned around.

"Theo, could you come with me to this interview? It's a possible witness but also a possible suspect as well. I think it should be a two-man job."

Theo looked as though he wanted to refuse but, technically, Kate was now his senior officer. Frowning, he nodded and got up from his desk.

"Unless you've got something for Nicola that you need to be doing that's more urgent?"

Kate meant this quite genuinely but the second the words were out of her mouth, she realised how Theo might construe it. His face went even redder and he mumbled something that she couldn't quite hear. "Great, great," she said hurriedly. "Let's go then."

Once they were sat in the car, Kate took another deep breath and turned to her colleague.

"Theo, I'm not going to beat around the bush. I'm really sorry for what happened and I—I just wanted to say that obviously, it's none of my business, but I won't tell anybody. I won't get you into trouble."

Theo exhaled and slumped back in his chair, closing his eyes. There was a short pause. "Thanks, mate," he said, eventually.

Kate hesitated. "Well...we can leave it there if you want." She looked more closely at Theo, noting the dark circles under his eyes and the stubble that looked as though it had been growing for a few days. "Unless... Unless you *want* to talk about it?"

Theo gave her a sideways glance and then looked away. "Um—"

"It's okay," said Kate. "It's none of my business. But, you know, I have been there." She gave him a smile. "And it worked out okay for me."

Theo smiled back. "Yeah, I know. I dunno... I really like her but—well, you know... She's the boss of me. Literally."

Kate turned the key in the ignition. "I know."

"And...we shouldn't really be doing this."

"I know that, too."

Theo slumped again. "So that's me, rock and a hard place."

Kate would have normally made some sort of smutty joke at this point in the conversation, but she had a feeling it wouldn't be appreciated at this moment in time. "Well, what are you going to do?"

Theo put a hand up to his head as if it hurt him. "I don't *know*."

"All right," said Kate, sensing that an argument was just around the corner. "Let's leave it for now. I'm sure things will work themselves out." She thought for a moment and added "And I really will keep it to myself, I promise."

"Thanks, mate."

They drove in silence for a few miles. Then Theo seemed to shake himself back to the job in hand and asked, "So, what can you tell me about this suspect?"

"I don't know that she *is* a suspect," said Kate. "But she's linked to at least two of the crime scenes. She was at the children's care home that William

Bathford ran. Her social worker, at least for a while, was Amanda Callihan." Kate clenched the wheel as a thought occurred to her. "Theo, ring the office and get someone to find the link between Roland Barry and William Bathford."

"Is there one?" Theo reached for his phone.

"There will be, I'm certain of it. He was a teacher, wasn't he? Perhaps he taught at the care home."

"Okay," Theo said dubiously. "But I'm sure that would have been flagged up before, wouldn't it?"

"I don't know." Kate tapped the wheel impatiently. "Things get missed, don't they?"

"Alright, alright, I'm on it." Theo tapped at his phone's screen and held it to his ear.

Chapter Twenty Two

KATE WAS KEENLY AWARE THAT she had a tendency to judge people. Although years of experience should have taught her that people were more than stereotypes, she had to fight with herself not to pre-judge people when she knew their background and histories. She knew Melanie Smith had grown up in care and had been in and out of trouble with the law throughout her adult life. Kate reminded herself that people could transcend their backgrounds. God knew, she had done it herself. So, as she and Theo approached a rundown block of flats surrounded by a small warren of council houses, Kate reminded herself that Melanie could very well be well-groomed, well-spoken, somebody whom you wouldn't have expected to grow up in care. *Just say what you mean, Kate. Not a member of the underclass.* Wincing inwardly, Kate shook herself mentally and focused her attention on the present.

It therefore came as a small shock when Melanie answered the door of her small terraced house, smoking cigarette in her hand, greasy hair dragged back from her worn face in a Croydon facelift, wearing stained tracksuit trousers and filthy Ugg boots.

"Yeah?" she said, suspiciously.

Kate and Theo flashed their credentials. Melanie didn't react with the kind of shock they were used to seeing. She frowned and asked what they wanted.

"We're investigating the deaths of Roland Barry, Amanda Cahill and William Bathford," said Kate. "Could we come in for a moment?"

Melanie looked as if she was going to refuse. Then, shrugging heavy shoulders, she turned and left the door open for them.

Kate and Theo walked into a tip, a home where clutter threatened to overwhelm the battered furniture. Smoke hung in the air like a grey curtain. A soiled nappy was bundled together on the carpet by the gas fire and plastic toys were heaped in untidy piles everywhere. Kate was suddenly transported back to her childhood; to the noise, the chaos, the embarrassment. Repressing a shudder, she sat gingerly on the edge of an armchair.

"You got kids, Mrs Smith?" asked Theo, looking around the room.

"Yeah, four of 'em. They're at school and nursery." Melanie sat down opposite Kate, shoving a pile of clothing off the sofa and onto the floor to make room for her ample behind. "And I'm not married."

Kate nodded. "Could we call you Melanie?"

Melanie shrugged but didn't demur.

"As I said before, we're investigating the deaths of Roland Barry, Amanda Cahill and William Bathford. Do any of those names mean anything to you, Melanie?"

Melanie lit another cigarette from the stub of the first. "No."

Kate sighed inwardly. "Have a think, Melanie."

"I said *no*." Melanie turned her head away as if offended by the very sight of Kate. Then she froze. "Wait, what was the last one?"

"William Bathford," said Kate, watching her closely.

Melanie's face contracted for a second. "Bathford— he's dead?"

"Yes, he died a couple of years ago." Kate added "In very suspicious circumstances."

Melanie drew on the cigarette as if it were administering life-saving oxygen. "Bathford. That bastard."

"So, you did know him, then?"

Melanie threw her a look of scorn. "You know I did, otherwise you wouldn't be here, right?"

Kate leaned forward. "So, tell us about him, Melanie?"

"Am I under arrest, or what?"

"Not yet," said Theo. "But I suggest you start talking."

It was a long, rambling recounting. Melanie spoke, mostly keeping her eyes on the floor, chain-smoking throughout. Her free hand kept going up to her ponytail, pulling on it and tightening the hairband.

Kate and Theo listened in silence, only prompting her a few times when her words dried up. It was the usual sad story: no father in the picture, mother died young, no family to take Melanie in. "I was in care my whole childhood," she mumbled. "Got fostered once or twice but it never lasted."

"I'm sorry," said Kate, who genuinely was.

Melanie sniffed. "Yeah, well. That Bathford—" She hesitated.

Kate and Theo exchanged glances. "Go on, Melanie," said Kate.

Melanie lit another cigarette. Kate thought, with an inner sigh, of all the washing she would have to do once home. Every piece of clothing she was wearing was going to reek of smoke.

"Yeah, well, Bathford, he started paying me a bit more attention. You know, giving me sweets and letting me watch TV in his room and all that."

Kate nodded, not wanting to interrupt her.

Melanie coughed. "It were grooming, I know that now, but when I were fourteen, you don't know, do you? You just like the attention."

Kate decided to ask directly. "Melanie, are you saying that William Bathford sexually abused you?"

Melanie didn't blush. Her face tightened. "Yeah," she said, after a moment.

"So, the allegations that you made to the Whitehaven police were true?"

169

Melanie nodded. She ground her cigarette out into the brimming ashtray with a vicious twist.

Kate tried to say it gently. "So, why did you withdraw those allegations?"

Melanie rubbed at her eyes. She was silent so long that Theo coughed restlessly. Kate shot him a warning glance.

Eventually Melanie spoke. "He—Bathford—he told me nobody would believe me. He scared me, telling me all about the courts and stuff. Like, I'd be totally humiliated in front of everyone. And—" She stopped for a moment, a crack in her voice. "He... I wasn't exactly sure it was wrong, what we were doing. Because, he told me I was his special girl, you know. Like his girlfriend."

Kate nodded. Dirty and dishevelled as Melanie was, for a moment Kate wanted nothing more than to hug her. She could see that scared, confused child in Melanie's hardened face. "I understand, Melanie, I totally understand." She paused and added, "And what about Karen Black?"

Melanie looked directly at her. "Who?"

"The other girl who reported William Bathford at the same time as you did."

Melanie sniffed again. "Oh, her. I dunno."

"Do you think she was telling the truth, too?"

Melanie's words came out in a cloud of exhaled smoke. "I dunno. She used to lie all the time, she was like a psycho."

Kate leaned forward. "Tell me about her. Anything that you remember, please."

Melanie shrugged. "I don't remember much about her. She punched one boy in the face once. She used to cut herself all up the arms, she had real problems."

"It sounds like it." Kate glanced about the room, wondering if there was any way in hell that Melanie would have a photograph of herself or of Karen Black back when they were teenagers. Was it even worth asking?

Then she froze. Her gaze snagged on something on top of a battered looking cupboard over in the corner, almost lost in the clutter of toys, papers, clothes and empty Coke cans surrounding it. Kate got up and walked over to it, glancing back at Theo, who had also stiffened.

"Melanie, where did you get this?" Kate reached into her bag, where she always kept a pair of surgical gloves. She snapped one on and picked up the statue of the woman. It was slightly different to the Erinyes they had found at the recent crime scenes; more crudely carved, less detailed, made of a different type of stone. Kate held it up in front of Melanie. "Where did you get this?" she repeated.

Melanie's eyes flickered. "I dunno. Can't remember."

Kate and Theo exchanged a glance. "Come on, Melanie, you need to try and recall. It's very important," said Kate.

"I told you, I can't remember."

"Did you make it?"

Melanie scoffed. "As if. I've had it for ages, dunno where I got it."

She's lying. Kate sighed inwardly and glanced again at Theo, who nodded slightly.

Kate turned back to Melanie. "Melanie Smith, I'm arresting you for the murder of William Bathford, Roland Barry and Amanda Cahill." She followed this with the usual words of the caution. Melanie looked bewildered, rather than angry. "Come on, we're taking you to the station."

Melanie blinked rapidly. "What about me kids?"

"Have you anyone you can call to collect them from school?" Kate's glance fell on the bundled nappy on the carpet. "Or nursery?"

"No. The mums at school don't like me."

"We'll make sure Social Services deal with it. They can arrange temporary foster care."

"No doubt they know you already," said Theo. Melanie didn't look as though she'd taken that in, but Kate winced inwardly. Theo was probably right but a pointed remark like that was just kicking someone when they were down. She fought the urge to give him a poke in the ribs. "Come on, Melanie. It'll be fine."

Theo was already bagging the statue. I'll have to get a warrant, thought Kate. This whole house will have to be searched. *Oh help, that means I have to face Nicola...*

Well, it couldn't be helped. She led Melanie out to the car while Theo dialled the number for Social Services.

Chapter Twenty Three

"GET FORENSICS ON THAT STATUE," Kate snapped at Theo as they arrived back in the office. He rolled his eyes.

"Mate, I'm on it, okay?"

"I'm your DI, not your mate." Kate saw Chloe's eyebrows go up in shock and Theo's face register her words. She bit down on the apology that wanted to follow.

"Right," said Theo, after a moment, and bore the evidence bag off accompanied by a dark frown.

Chloe looked at Kate as if she'd grown an extra head. "Bird, you okay?"

"I'm fine." Nervously stretched as she was, Kate couldn't give Chloe the same treatment. "This is the breakthrough, this is where we find the evidence."

Chloe sat down in her chair and looked steadily at Kate. "Why do you say that?"

It was Kate's turn to roll her eyes. "Hello? Same statue as found at all the murder scenes? Melanie lying about how long she's had it and where she got it?"

Chloe's gaze didn't waver. "Why, if she's guilty, would she not have hidden it away?"

Kate shuffled some papers on her desk. "She's not that clever?"

"Come *on*..."

Kate looked up into Chloe's eyes. "I don't know. She's *not* that clever. It's a link, though, Chloe, can't you see that?"

"Yeah, I see that. But—" Chloe broke off her sentence and turned her eyes to her keyboard.

Kate knew what Chloe was saying was right but, perversely, that only made her angrier. "Well, seeing as we're weeks into two separate investigations and we haven't got so much as a motive, let alone a suspect, I think this is worth prioritising."

"I'm sure you're right." Chloe's voice was cool.

Silence fell. Kate sniffed and, after a minute, pushed back her chair. She headed for the kitchenette, needing coffee like she needed oxygen.

Staring at the kettle as it boiled, Kate thought about what had happened. Chloe was right. Why would Melanie keep the statue in plain sight if she was the one leaving them at the murder scenes? Was it a case of a magnificent double-bluff? Kate recalled Melanie, her troubled past, her inadequacies, her dishevelment. She recalled her own words to Chloe. *Weeks into two separate investigations and we haven't got so much as a motive, let alone a suspect.* Surely Melanie didn't have the intelligence to outwit the entire coterie of the Abbeyford force?

The kettle clicked off and Kate prepared her

drink. After a moment's thought, she made one for Chloe and for Theo, too. She carried his over to his desk where he was bashing away at his keyboard as if it had personally offended him.

"Sorry," said Kate, handing him his mug. Theo looked up, startled.

"Thanks."

"I'm being a dick. Sorry."

Theo grinned. "Hormones, probably."

Kate grinned back even as she punched him gently on the arm. Then she took Chloe her drink and said much the same thing.

"It's okay," Chloe said awkwardly. "You were right."

Kate slumped back into her chair. "The statue. What are the chances it has any fingerprints on it at all? Suppose she's had it for years or made it years ago?"

"Well, we can but try," Chloe soothed. "Forensics are good. If there's anything to be found, they'll find it."

"I know." Kate took a sip of her drink. "There *was* something..."

She trailed off. Chloe was looking at her expectantly.

"What, bird?"

"I don't know." Kate put her mug back down. "Something... Something tickling me. Something I've seen that could be relevant."

She fell silent. Chloe waited and then, on Kate's ensuing silence, shrugged. "It'll come back to you."

"I know." Kate *did* know. These flashes of intuition had served her well in the past. Of course, half of them had come to nothing as well...

She shook herself back to reality and got up, bracing herself. Then she walked down to DCI Weaver's office and knocked on the door.

Once facing Nicola across her desk, Kate made a real effort to appear utterly focused on what she was about to tell her. Nicola did not blush, but her face was a little tighter than normal. Despite herself, Kate was impressed by the way she made eye-contact and held Kate's gaze steadily.

"Sit down, Kate."

Silently relieved that she hadn't been demoted back to 'DI Redman' (or worse, 'DS Redman'), Kate lowered herself into the chair. "We have a suspect in custody for both murders."

Nicola's well-shaped eyebrows rose. "Indeed?"

Kate gave her the run-down on the arrest of Melanie Smith and the discovery of the statue. "It's on the twenty-four-hour turnaround for fingerprints and any other evidence. I didn't know whether you wanted me to interview Melanie? She's being allocated one of the duty solicitors."

Nicola steepled her fingers under her chin in a way startlingly reminiscent of Anderton. She was silent for a few moments. "Do you have a warrant yet for the house search?"

"It's in hand. We'll start as soon as we have it."

Nicola nodded. Then she unlaced her fingers and dropped her hands to the desk. "Thank you for your efforts, Kate. I'll interview the suspect."

Slightly taken aback, it was Kate's turn to nod. DCI Weaver didn't often do interviews. It was a measure of how seriously she was taking this case, Kate supposed. "Fine." She wondered whether to mention that flash of intuition she'd felt but dismissed it. It was too nebulous to name. "Supervise the house search for me. See if you can find anything, anything at all, that will link our suspect to either of the victims."

Inwardly grimacing at the thought of rummaging through Melanie's slovenly house, Kate agreed to. Dismissed by her DCI, she walked back to her desk, wondering if this task had been given to her as a mild punishment, a pointed remark as to hold her tongue on what she'd witnessed. *Such paranoia, Kate.*

Chloe was busy scanning the screen of her computer and making frantic notes. Kate waved to get her attention. "Want to come and do a house search with me? Melanie Smith's place?"

"I thought you hadn't got the warrant yet?"

"Nicola will have signed it off by the time I get there."

Chloe pouted. "Sorry, bird, but I've been given my orders. Trying to find a link between Bathford and Barry."

"No problem." Kate straightened up and scanned the room. If only Olbeck were here...but she was being foolish. Two DIs would be wasted on a house search. She made a mental note to call her friend later and approached Rav, asking him the same question she'd put to Chloe.

"Sorry, Kate, I've got CCTV to watch and a ton of paperwork to do."

Kate nodded. She looked more closely at her colleague, noting the dark circles under his eyes. "You okay, Rav? You look knackered."

"I'm okay. Just tired." He looked down at his hands, gold wedding ring glinting under the office lights. "I had to take Jarina to the A and E last night, so we got home really late."

Kate felt a clutch in her stomach. "Oh, Rav. Oh, God, is she okay?" She leant forward to drop her voice. "Is the baby okay?"

"They think so. They're keeping her in overnight just to check."

"Oh Rav..." Kate fought the urge to give him a hug. "You must be worried sick."

Rav's mouth twitched. "Yeah, I am."

Kate looked around to see if anyone was in earshot. "Don't you need to be with her?"

"*I* thought so. I told her that, but she said her mum was coming and I needed to go to work."

"Oh, well." Kate tried to smile supportively. "I'm sure it'll be fine. If you need any help, you just let me know, okay?" She looked around again and added, conspiratorially, "Why don't you slip off early? I can say you've got an interview to do, or something."

Rav smiled. "I might do that. Thanks, Kate."

Kate gave him a pat on the shoulder and headed back to her desk. She'd have to pick up a few uniformed officers to accompany her but that could be arranged. Head fizzing with a thousand thoughts, she picked up her office phone and dialled the front desk.

Chapter Twenty Four

MELANIE SMITH'S HOUSE WAS A small, two-bed terrace, one of thousands of social housing units that had been thrown up in the nineteen sixties and seventies. She was lucky, thought Kate, to have got a council house. Single parents seeking accommodation on benefits now would be lucky to find a privately rented flat whose landlord would take housing benefit or universal credit. The house was utterly nondescript, the tiny front garden paved in concrete which was slippery and green with moss.

Kate and her two companions, PC Sarah Renton and PC Josh Gadding, gloved up at the door. Kate was more than usually grateful for a thin layer of plastic between her hands and whatever it was she was going to discover. She chided herself. *If you were a single mother, brought up in care, no money, four children, no support...* Kate doubted that keeping an immaculate show home was top of your priorities.

Still... As the officers began to spread out through the house and turn their attention to the search, Kate was finding it hard not to judge. Ashtrays were everywhere, clotted with cigarette stubs and grey ash. The kitchen cupboards disgorged a plethora of cider bottles, both full and empty. Kate gave thanks that it was autumn, shading to winter—the thought of this kitchen, with its mounds of unwashed dishes and uncovered, rotting food, in the high summer was stomach-churning. A single child's drawing was anchored to the fridge with a *Keep Calm and Carry On* magnet. Kate read the wartime phrase printed on the cheap plastic. It seemed strangely apt.

The only thing different was the children's bedroom. Three of them shared a room, with two bunk beds and a cot bed crammed into the small space. But someone—surely Melanie—had tried to brighten the walls with alphabet stickers and a rug with coloured stars printed upon it. The room was a mess, but it was a homely mess.

Kate cleared the blockage in her throat with a cough and knelt on the carpet. She hated searching children's rooms; it seemed like such an intrusion. But unfortunately, in many cases, it was where they found the evidence. She heaved up small mattresses, feeling beneath, carefully lifted jumbles of brightly coloured clothing into neat stacks onto the floor, and went through the one chest of drawers into the room, sliding her hand across the underside of each drawer. The bunkbeds were made of wood—cheap flatpack, as was the cotbed—so nothing to be hidden inside the head or footboard. Having found nothing but a decomposing chocolate bar beneath the bunkbed, Kate could tick the room off with relief.

She moved back into the narrow upstairs corridor. Busy noises of furniture being moved could be heard downstairs. As Kate was about to shout "Anything?" to her companions, the doorbell went, announcing the arrival of the scene of crime team.

Stephen Smithfield was heading the team, as usual. "Kate," he greeted her. "General sweep, is it?"

"Yep. Fingerprints particularly."

Stephen looked around him with eyebrows raised. "Well, I think you might be in luck, Kate. Doesn't look like a lot of cleaning goes on around here, does it?"

"She's got four children," said Kate.

"Messy little buggers," agreed Stephen. "Righto, we'll get on with it."

Kate moved into Melanie's bedroom, which she shared with her youngest child, evidenced by another cot pushed up against her single bed. Kate worked methodically, lifting the mattresses of both beds, examining the underside. There was a single chest of drawers in the room and Kate went through it drawer by drawer. There was a plastic bag with some weedy remnants of marijuana at the bottom of it, and some rolling papers, but Kate didn't raise her eyebrows much at that. She bagged it as evidence anyway, although she was doubtful it would ever be used. The rest of the drawers yielded nothing but cheap and badly made clothes.

The only other possible hiding place was a collapsing cardboard box in the corner of the room. Kate hauled it over to beneath the window, to maximise the light. She lifted out various forms and documents; letters from Social Services, loan statements. There were various old birthday cards. Right at the bottom were some photographs. Kate carefully lifted them out and examined them. Most were of what seemed to be a young Melanie, quite startlingly pretty, given how she looked now. There was only one that made Kate pause. She lifted it closer to her face. It was a landscape shot, of what she now knew to be the Carndale care home.

Kate bagged all the photographs. They proved nothing, except that Melanie had been at the Carndale care home, which was common knowledge anyway. But, you never knew what might come in handy in an investigation...

She was walking down the stairs when her mobile rang. It was Chloe.

"Bird? Forensics have come back on the statue."

"That was quick," said Kate, surprised but pleased. "Well?"

"Well, there's a fingerprint match on the statue to one Karen Black."

"Her fingerprints are on file?" Kate clenched her fist in frustration. "Had no one even done a search for them?"

Chloe sounded embarrassed. "Well, no. It was on the list of things to do."

"Christ—" Kate checked herself, asking herself why she hadn't bothered to check. "Okay, so what's she on file for?"

"This is a long time ago—years ago—but she was arrested for assault in 2003, during a fight in a pub in Northampton. She was in the army at the time; it was a squaddies' pub."

"Karen Black was in the army?" Kate clenched her fist again, this time in exhilaration. "Great, so we can trace her. Get onto that, Chloe, and I'll come back to the office."

"Have you found anything?"

"Nothing very important. I'll see you soon." Kate said goodbye and dropped her mobile back into her handbag.

***

AFTER A BREAK, THE INTERVIEW with Melanie Smith continued into the night. Melanie had been assigned one of the duty solicitors, a very attractive young woman. Kate, taking her seat on the opposite side of the table, next to DCI Weaver, remembered that Theo normally tried to get into every interview in which this lawyer was present. But then, considering his lover was heading the investigation, perhaps it wasn't so surprising that he wasn't there.

"I need to talk to you about Karen Black," said DCI Weaver.

Melanie's sullen gaze was on the table. "I told you, I don't know her. I haven't seen her for years."

"Her fingerprint was found on the statue we took from your home, Melanie."

"So?"

"So, how did it get there if you haven't seen her for years?"

Melanie looked up. She spoke through clenched teeth. "I told you, *I don't know her.*"

The duty solicitor shifted slightly in her seat and whispered in Melanie's ear. Kate could imagine what it was she was saying. She sighed inwardly, braced for Melanie to enter the 'no comment' zone.

What happened surprised her. Melanie looked at her solicitor and shook her head, fiercely. "Look, I'll tell you, okay? I just want to get back to my kids."

Both Kate and Nicola tensed slightly. "Go on, Melanie," said Nicola.

"Can I have a fag?"

"There's no smoking in here, I'm afraid."

Melanie slumped back into her seat, frowning. "Look, Karen gimme that statue, but when we were kids, right? She used to make them, it was like a hobby for her."

Thank you, Melanie. Kate felt a leap of excitement at her words. "Go on," was what she said.

"She give it me when we were at the home. After

I said I'd back her up, you know, with the police and all."

Nicola raised her eyebrows. "So, Karen gave you the statue when you were at the children's home together. You were good friends, then?"

Melanie screwed up her face. "Nah, not really. But she was pleased, you know, when I said I'd back her up."

It was Kate's turn to speak. "But you let her down, Melanie, didn't you? You withdrew your allegation and the investigation collapsed."

Melanie looked at her with dislike. "Look, I *told* you I didn't know what I was doing, I was under a lot of pressure. I was fifteen, for fuck's sake."

Kate nodded. "How did Karen react when you told her you were withdrawing those allegations?"

"How do you think? She went crazy. Tried to hit me. One of the workers pulled her off me."

"She must have been extremely angry."

Melanie's gaze dropped. "Yeah. Well, I could sort of see it from her point of view."

Kate made a note in her notebook. "So, what happened then?"

Melanie shrugged. "That was the last time I saw her. She ran away the next day and never came back."

"And you've never seen her again?" Kate leant forward to watch the expression on Melanie's face.

Melanie's gaze flickered minutely. "No, never. I never saw her again."

It was Nicola and Kate's turned to exchange a

glance. Kate was almost certain Melanie was lying, but it was going to be hard to prove it.

Nicola spoke to pause the interview and inclined her head towards the door. Kate nodded.

Outside, Nicola and Kate faced one another.

"What do you make of her?" asked Nicola.

"She's lying about not seeing Karen since. *Probably* lying."

"Yes, I think you're right." Nicola flicked a stray hair from her face and smoothed her hand down over her hair. "I'm going to carry on grilling her. Kate, can you do all you can to help the others track Karen Black down? She, along with Melanie, is currently our prime suspect."

"Of course." A previous case occurred to Kate. "It wouldn't... They wouldn't be working together on this, would they?"

"It's a possibility," said Nicola.

"Does Melanie have an alibi for any of the crimes?"

Nicola looked grim. "Her children can apparently alibi her for Roland Barry's murder. I'm still ascertaining her whereabouts when Amanda Cahill was killed."

Kate prepared to say goodbye. Then something else struck her. "That's one good thing. We've got it in her own words that Karen Black makes those statues. No wonder Rav couldn't track down the manufacturer."

"That's if she's telling the truth about that."

"True," admitted Kate. Again, she felt that

flicker of intuition, that annoying twitch of some subconscious memory. She strained to grasp it but, within a moment, it had gone once more. Kate sighed. "I'll get started with Karen Black."

"Good." That was the highest praise Kate had ever had from her DCI. Nicola gave her a crisp smile and then went back into the interview room, shutting the door.

Chapter Twenty Five

"You got anything yet?" Kate leaned over Chloe's shoulder to look at what her computer screen was showing.

"Nothing concrete. I'm trying to trace her former regiment."

"I'll do some checking as well." Kate sat back down at her own desk and fired up several databases on her computer. As she was waiting for them to load, her gaze fell on Rav's desk, empty of him. Troubled, she picked up her phone and tapped out a text. *Everything okay with J? X.*

Chloe gave an exclamation of satisfaction. Kate looked up. "Got something?"

"A phone number. Shush, while I make this call?"

Kate obediently zipped it, the merest thought of the fact that, as a DI, she didn't warrant being subdued pushed to the back of her mind. She listened to Chloe begin to make her preparatory enquiries and then dragged her attention back to her own computer screen. Her mobile chimed and she picked it up to see that Rav had messaged her back. *All okay, thanks mate. We're back at home X.*

One worry off her mind, Kate dropped the phone into her handbag and looked at her computer screen. She could hear Chloe talking with whomever she was speaking with on the other end of the line and tried not to listen in.

Eventually, Chloe put the receiver down and looked across at Kate.

"Something?" Kate asked, trying not to sound too eager.

"He's sending across what he's got now." Chloe tapped at her keyboard. "Here we go..."

Kate raced around to Chloe's side of the desk and both of them held their breath as the attachment to the email downloaded. As the pixels on the screen gradually coalesced into a coherent picture, Kate breathed out heavily.

"What?" Chloe looked up at her.

Kate leant forward, her eyes fixed on the screen. The woman's picture showed a heavy-browed, short-haired woman, facing the camera. "I know that face," Kate breathed out.

"You're joking."

"No, I'm not. I've seen her before. Somewhere." Kate fixed her gaze on the woman's face, as though if she broke her stare, she might forget the likeness. "*Where* have I seen that face before?"

Chloe took a look. "I don't recognise her. She looks tough, though, hey?"

"Our prime suspect." Kate reached a finger out to

touch the woman's forehead on the screen. "Oh, God, *where* have I seen her? That's going to drive me mad."

"Someone you've interviewed? Arrested?"

"Perhaps."

"Someone you've seen a long time ago, or recently?"

Kate shook her head, as if trying to dislodge the memory and set it free. "Recently, I think..." She sat back down in her chair abruptly and flung herself back in despair. "I just can't remember."

"There, there," soothed Chloe. "It'll come back to you. Besides, now I might be able to track her down anyway."

"Sure," said Kate. "You get on it, and I'll go and tell Nicola what we've got." She thought for a moment and then added, "Why not go and see her ex-commander in chief, or whatever the term is? The bloke you've just been talking to. They'll be able to tell you quite a lot."

Chloe nodded, pursing her lips. She hit the 'redial' button on her phone and covered the mouthpiece with her hand as she waited for someone to answer. "Are you going to come along once I get hold of him?"

Kate toyed with the idea before quickly deciding against it. That sort of task didn't warrant the attendance of two officers. I'm learning to delegate, she thought with pride as she shook her head and gave Chloe a 'good luck' thumbs up.

As Chloe began to speak to whoever was on the end of the line, Kate looked down at her notes. What now? She could see by looking at her emails that

Chloe had already distributed the photograph of Karen Black to the team. Again, Kate was struck by the very faint feeling of familiarity as she looked at it. Kate was good with faces; most police officers were. Names not so much, she thought, with an inner grin. Again came that faint flicker of intuition, the whisper of memory that continued to elude her.

Sighing, she got up and made her way to Nicola's office, determined to leave a note if her boss was still stuck in Melanie Smith's interview. To Kate's surprise, Nicola was just exiting her office and shutting the door behind her.

"I thought you'd still be interviewing," Kate said, raising a hand in greeting.

Nicola exhaled sharply and shook her smooth head. "We're giving her a ten minute break. I'll be back in there shortly." She paused and added, rather grimly, "She's reached the 'no comment' stage by now, anyway. I'm not going to get very much more out of her."

Kate nodded in understanding. "Are you going to charge her?"

Nicola's frown deepened. "I don't see that we can. We've got nothing—nothing but an admission that the two girls knew each other back when they were teenagers. That and a fingerprint on a statue that Melanie freely admits Karen gave to her."

"It's not much," agreed Kate. "The CPS wouldn't even take it on with just that."

"Exactly. We're running out of time to charge her anyway, and I doubt I'll be able to get an extension."

This was the easiest, most free-flowing conversation that Kate had ever had with her DCI. She opened her mouth and began "Can I see you for just a mo—"

"Sorry, Kate." Nicola was shifting from foot to foot. "I am *desperate* for the loo. Wait in my office, and I'll be back shortly."

"Right, no problem." Kate watched as Nicola hurried off down the corridor. *The old girl is thawing out, wonder of wonders.* She opened the office door and went in to sit down. *Perhaps Theo really is a demon lover after all.* She started laughing at the thought. *Dammit, I should have tried him out while I had the chance...*

Giggling to herself, she let her eyes roam about the room. There were several healthy-looking house plants, lush and green, but very few personal touches. The only photograph that Kate could see was of Nicola and an older woman, one who looked enough like her for Kate to assume that it was a mother-daughter shot. She realised how little she knew about her boss; whether she was married, whether she had children, where she'd grown up. Not that Nicola had ever volunteered the information but then Kate hadn't ever bothered to ask.

Feeling slightly guilty, she let her gaze drift further from the photograph to a little white soapstone statue in the shape of the Buddha with a tiny brass plate placed in front of it. So, Nicola was a Buddhist, was she? Kate snorted at the thought. Of course, it could be she just liked the statue and it had no religious connotations at all...

Statue...

DCI Weaver came back into the room just as Kate sat bolt upright in her chair and let out an audible yelp.

"Kate?" said Nicola, puzzled.

"I remember! I know! I know where I've seen the statue!"

Nicola looked at her as if she'd gone mad. "What? What statue?"

"The Buddha statue. That was what I kept thinking of, but I couldn't remember—I couldn't put my finger on what it was." The second Kate said the words, she realised where she'd seen Karen Black's face. She dropped back in her chair, as if feeling faint, and covered her face with her hands. "Oh my god. I know who she is."

"Who, for God's sake?"

Predictably and infuriatingly, Kate had forgotten her name. She said as much. "Dammit, she's the therapist, the life coach at the yoga studios where Amanda Callihan taught. Oh Christ, what was her name?"

"It doesn't matter. That's soon ascertainable. Listen, Kate, are you sure?"

"Yes, yes, I am. Oh God, the *relief*. That's been nagging me for days—"

Nicola was no longer listening. She was already dialling a number on her office phone.

Chapter Twenty Six

TWO HOURS LATER, THE ABBEYFORD team faced one another across the office. Everyone was there, even Rav, who had returned from ensuring his wife was comfortable at home. Despite the tense atmosphere, Kate gave him a surreptitious thumbs-up across the table, which he returned with a grin.

DCI Weaver paced the floor in front of the whiteboards in a way reminiscent of Anderton. "Now, I'll recap before we get going. Our prime suspect, Karen Black, has been located. She currently has the alias of Rachel Brown; she's practicing as a life coach in the rooms next to the studio where Amanda Callihan taught."

Kate heard Chloe suck in her breath beside her and smiled inwardly. Chloe hadn't ever heard the best of it.

Nicola carried on speaking. "Karen Black, AKA Rachel Brown, was also, briefly, Amanda Callihan's therapist, or counsellor. We're in the process of chasing down her current abode, but I'm sending a small team to investigate her offices at the studio." Nicola paused and added, "The team will be accompanied by an ARU."

ARU. Armed Response Unit. Kate could feel how high the stakes were getting and, judging by the lightning fast glances between them, the other team members could too.

DCI Weaver looked Kate in the eye. "Kate, I want you to head the team." Kate nodded tensely. Nicola's gaze moved onto Theo, who dropped his own to the floor. "DS—I mean, Theo, I want you to accompany DI Redman." She swung back round to face Chloe and Rav. "DS Wapping, DS Cheetham, I want you to pull out all the stops to try and track down Karen Black's current whereabouts. Pull in uniform if you have to." Another pause and her gaze swept the room. "Am I understood?"

A murmur of "Yes, DCI Weaver," resounded and then Nicola was gone from the room, striding through the doorway with the words, "I'll be in my office if anyone needs me," trailing behind her.

There was a collective and audible exhalation of breath at her departure, but it was a different flavour to the usual sigh of irritation that DCI Weaver's exit usually provoked. Chloe looked at Kate and raised her eyebrows. "Here we go, eh, bird?"

"Here we go." Kate gestured to Theo, who swept his jacket onto his shoulders. "Let's go. You got the address, right?"

"Good luck, guys," called Rav as they hurried

from the office. Kate gave him another thumbs up in response.

"What about the ARU?" Theo gasped as they pounded down the stairs.

"Meeting us round the corner from the studio," Kate said, pushing open the door to the carpark. She'd been through all of this in a private briefing with DCI Weaver. "I'm driving."

Theo didn't protest. Soon, they were in Kate's car and speeding towards the centre of Abbeyford. Remembering the problems she'd had with parking there before, Kate headed straight for one of the central carparks and left her car there. She and Theo walked quickly towards the side-street where they'd agreed to rendezvous with the armed unit.

Experienced as she was, Kate never found dealing with armed police officers easy. As they exchanged terse greetings, she remembered her first sergeant, Alan Whittock, telling her that if the law changed and it came to pass that every officer in Britain would be armed, he would immediately resign. "We police by consent, not by force," he'd said. Kate tipped the memory of him a respectful mental salute.

"We'll go in first," said the head of the ARU, Gavin Rinstock. He was a stocky, silver-haired man in his forties.

"Yes, I know," said Kate. "When can we follow?"

"When I give the all clear. Wait here."

Internally rolling her eyes, Kate nodded and

stepped back. Theo, clearly chomping at the bit to join in, jogged from foot to foot.

"Calm down," said Kate. They watched as the squad ran towards the building.

"Oh, man," said Theo. "I'm applying for a transfer. That's what I want to do."

"Seriously?" Kate raised her eyebrows. "Why?"

"I want a big gun. And, you know, to run into buildings and blow shit up and stuff."

Kate's eyeballs were beginning to hurt from the rolling. "*Seriously*? This isn't Hollywood, Theo."

"I know." Theo smiled sheepishly. "But, you know, maybe it's time for a change."

Kate straightened up. "Are you serious?"

"I don't know."

They looked at each other. Kate scanned Theo's face, a face she'd seen every week for years. She looked at him now with fresh eyes. He was no longer the pretty-faced young thing she'd once contemplated a fling with. Still as good looking, his face had broadened and his hair was greying. She had a flashback to watching Andrew Stanton performing that post-mortem and realising his once-red hair was now silver. Everything's changing, she thought. *We're all getting old.*

"Seriously—" She caught herself. "Okay, I keep saying the same thing. But Theo...really? Are you serious? You want to leave?"

"Not leave..." Theo looked down at the ground. "It's

just…everything's kind of up in the air at the moment. I don't know…you know, what's happening with—you know—"

Kate blew out her cheeks. "I know what you mean, mate. I really do."

They confronted each other. "What's going on with you and Anderton?" asked Theo.

Kate lifted her shoulders. "I don't know."

"What do you want to happen?"

Of all the likely scenarios, getting relationship advice from Theo was the last thing Kate had expected. "I don't know," was all she could come up with.

"It's—"Theo began and then they heard the crash of the front door of the yoga studios as it hit the floor.

"Perhaps another time for this conversation?" suggested Kate.

"Yeah." Theo spun around. "They're in. Let's go."

"They said to wait for the all clear—"Kate called after Theo's back as he ran towards the studio. "Look, just *wait*, would you?"

The ARU were quick and efficient. Within minutes, they had ascertained that the offices were empty, along with the yoga studios. When Kate heard the shout from Gavin Rinstock, she let go of Theo's arm, having been physically holding him back from entering. "Come on then, you lunatic."

They went straight to Karen's office and began the search. Theo bagged up the Buddha statue and held it up to the light. "You can see it's handmade from here." He looked across at Kate. "It's different to the ones left at the scenes, though, isn't it? What made you think of it?"

"I don't know. Call it intuition." Kate had gone straight to the filing cabinet. Within moments, she had located a credit card bill with an address on it in the name of Rachel Brown. "Theo, look." She took a photograph of the bill and texted it to Chloe. "Might be her current address. Chloe can start tracking her down."

"That's if she's there." Theo began to check the drawers of the desk. "She'll have gone into hiding, if she's got any sense."

"How optimistic." Kate riffled through a mass of client files. "God, I sometimes feel that all I've done on this case is look through paperwork..."

"It's always like that."

They continued the search. Kate's mobile chimed with a return text from Chloe. *Ta for address, bird. Rav's on it. I'm interviewing army bloke. PS. Melanie Smith being released for now* accompanied by a frowny faced emoji.

Kate sighed, annoyed but unsurprised. She relayed the new piece of information to Theo.

"Yeah, well, it's annoying but we know who and where she is now," said Theo. "Once we've got Karen Black in custody, we'll be pulling her in again, won't we?"

"No doubt."

***

By the time the search was complete, it was dark and raining incessantly. Wearily, Kate and Theo packed the boot of Kate's car with the collected evidence in bags and boxes. As they drove away, Kate could see the dim shape of a uniformed officer sitting in an unobtrusively parked car, watching out in case Karen decided to go back to her office. Giving thanks that her tailing days were over, Kate turned to Theo. "Are you going back to the office?"

"Nope, I'm bushed. Can you drop me home?"

"Sure." They drove to Theo's house in tired silence. As he was getting out, wincing at the rain, Kate held a hand out to his arm. "Listen, Theo, I'm sure things will work themselves out with—you know, with Nicola. If you ever need a friendly ear, you know where I am."

Theo looked grateful. "Thanks, mate. You're a good friend." He shook wet hair out of his eyes. "Besides, it worked out for you and Anderton, didn't it?"

"Yes, it did," Kate said, suddenly feeling more certain of the fact. "And I'm going to go and see him right now."

"Say hi from me."

"I will. Now get out of the rain."

Chuckling a little, Kate watched him run up the driveway of his house. Then she turned the windscreen wipers up to 'full' and drove away to Anderton's cottage.

Chapter Twenty Seven

CONSIDERING HOW WET THE PREVIOUS evening had been, Kate was pleasantly surprised to wake to golden autumnal sunshine the next morning. She lay in Anderton's arms, watching the dappling of light play on the bedroom wall.

"Thank you for that surprise visit last night," Anderton murmured in her ear.

"You're welcome. I was beginning to forget what you looked like."

"Well, that's hardly my fault, is it?"

Kate kissed him. "No, it's mine. And I know I'm going to be pulling a lot of late ones this week, so I thought I'd come over."

"Well, thank you."

Kate kissed him again, more lingeringly this time. Anderton slid a warm leg in between hers and pulled her closer.

She groaned. "I can't! I've got to go."

"Please. Just a quickie."

"I can't—"Kate said, in the tone of voice that she knew Anderton would take as saying 'well, not unless

CELINA GRACE

you persuade me'. She tried to say something else, but he covered her mouth with his. "Oh, go on then," she gasped, once she came up for air.

Later, driving to work, Kate reflected on the pleasant start to the morning with a smile on her face. Then she sighed a little. With work so intense, she had little headspace, or indeed the emotional energy, to devote some thought to where she and Anderton were going. *I really, really must talk to him properly, once this case is done.* She nodded to herself, made a mental note to do just that, and turned her attention back to the road.

Nicola was pacing the floor again when Kate got to the office. Wondering whether her DCI would make a sharp comment about her lateness (Kate was guiltily aware that her morning antics with Anderton had added another twenty minutes to her usual commute, quickie or no quickie), she smiled rather hesitantly at her boss.

"Kate, you're here. Good." It was said with no tone of sarcasm. "To bring you up to speed, we've raided Karen Black's home address. Thanks for getting that over to us so quickly, by the way."

Kate smiled again, pleased at the praise. "Have we got her yet?"

Nicola shook her head. "No, not that lucky, I'm afraid. I've got Rav and Theo over there now, gathering the evidence, of which I understand there's plenty."

"Oh yes?"

"Yes. All to the good when we build a case."

"Do you want me to go over there?"

Nicola shook her head. "No, they can handle it. I need you here, keeping everything turning. I've got a press conference in half an hour and I need you in the office."

"Sure." Kate was secretly relieved, having just got out of the car. "I'll crack on with things here, then."

"Thank you." Nicola gave her a distracted smile and hurried out. Just as quickly, she hurried back in. Kate looked up in surprise.

Nicola was looking awkward. "Kate, listen. I've—I've been meaning to say to you for a while how much I appreciate your—well—discretion. Over...well, you know—"

Astonished, Kate took a moment to respond. "It was none of my business."

"Well, I appreciate it." Nicola was almost scarlet now. Briefly Kate wondered whether she'd be able to resume her normal colour before she had to face the cameras.

"It's really not a problem," she said firmly.

Nicola gave her an embarrassed smile. "Well, thanks." Then she looked at the clock on the far wall and added, "Help, I must go. See you later."

She hurried off again. Raising her eyebrows—Kate had *not* been expecting that—she went over to her desk and tried to collect herself.

Once the press conference was underway, Kate

found the remote for the television over in the corner and turned it on. She found the right channel and watched as Nicola outlined the case for the media. She spoke well, and Kate found herself feeling oddly proud of her boss. It suddenly occurred to her that women now outnumbered the men in the office, with Olbeck away. Thinking of him, Kate sent a quick, supportive text to say hello and then slung her mobile in her bag, determined to get on with some work.

She was just checking through her emails when Chloe came into the office, sounding out of breath.

"You alright, bird?" asked Kate.

"Bloody car broke down again. I had to walk most of the way."

Kate groaned. "I thought you were getting rid of that old banger?"

"Well, it keeps going, most of the time."

Kate shook her head. "Anyway, it's okay. Nicola's doing a press release so you're safe."

Chloe was opening her mouth to respond when the phone on Kate's desk rang. She picked it up, wondering if this was going to be the call telling them that Karen Black had been apprehended.

"Kate, it's Jane Simmons here from the DSS."

"Hello," said Kate. She knew Jane slightly from working with the Department of Social Services. "What's the problem?" She crossed her fingers under the table that something horrible hadn't happened to a child.

Jane didn't sound upset, just rather puzzled. "Am I right in thinking that Melanie Smith is no longer in custody?"

"Yes, that's right. She was released yesterday."

Jane sounded even more puzzled. "Well, she was due to collect her children from the temporary foster home last night and, well, she didn't."

"She didn't? They're still there?"

"Yes. I mean, they're fine—the carers didn't tell them their mum was going to pick them up because, well, for all we know you could have charged her. So it's not that they were expecting her, but we were. She's not answering her mobile."

"That is strange," said Kate, thinking it was probably more likely that Melanie had seen the opportunity as a chance for some rare child-free time. But perhaps that was uncharitable. As she thought back, she remembered what Melanie had said. *Look, I'll tell you, okay? I just want to get back to my kids...* A twist of anxiety began to uncoil in her stomach. Out loud, she said, "We'll look into it, Jane, okay? We've got her address. You can leave it with us. Just make sure the kids can stay with their foster family for now."

"Of course."

"I'll keep you posted. Thanks, Jane." Kate said goodbye and hung up. She looked across the table at Chloe, who had clearly sensed the tension in her friend.

"What's wrong?" Chloe asked.

Kate rubbed her jaw in thought. "Melanie Smith appears to have gone missing."

"Seriously?"

"Well, she didn't turn up to collect her children when she was supposed to."

Chloe shrugged. "Well, she's hardly the reliable, conscientious type, is she? She's probably out on the razz or shacked up with some bloke while she's got the chance."

"Mmm." Even though those had been Kate's first thoughts, now she shook her head. "I don't know."

"Well, we can send some uniform over to her house to check, right?"

Kate stared into space, thinking. The worm of anxiety was bigger now, coiling and writhing. "I don't know, Chloe. I've got a bad feeling about this."

"Really?" Chloe looked sceptical. "Why?"

"I don't know just yet. Shut up and let me think."

Obediently, Chloe zipped it. Kate got up and began to walk around the office. She went over to the whiteboards and stared at the crime scene photographs, the victims, their faces. The statues. *The Furies*.

"Vengeance," she muttered. Then she gasped and swung round to face Chloe, who stood up immediately.

"What—" began Chloe.

Kate talked over her. "William Bathford—Karen's abuser. Roland Barry—her teacher, maybe. An abuser too, perhaps."

"Yes," said Chloe, staring at her.

"Amanda Callihan—the social worker who let her down."

"Yes, I suppose so."

Kate stared back at her. "Who else has let Karen Black down?"

Chloe frowned, puzzled. Then her face cleared. "Melanie Smith."

"Exactly. And by now Karen will know we're hunting her down."

"Christ." Chloe was already hunting for her jacket. "We'd better get over there."

"Someone needs to cover the office."

Chloe put up her eyebrows. "You're not going over there alone."

"I wouldn't. I'm taking armed back up."

"Let me organise that." Chloe flung herself back in her chair and reached for the phone. "I'll get someone else in here to deal with the phones, too."

"You do that," said Kate. She could feel her heart beating fast. "Thanks, bird."

She saw Chloe begin to dial a number and then she turned and ran, desperate to find Nicola.

Chapter Twenty Eight

THE LAST OF THE AFTERNOON light was draining from the sky as Kate, Chloe and their team made their way towards Melanie Smith's house. Chloe drove, which gave Kate the chance to think things through. Could she be right? Having spoken to Theo during this search of Karen Black's house, she knew that the evidence against her was overwhelming. But why had she started her campaign of vengeance now? Why not before? Had she really brooded and plotted for years, waiting to serve that dish of revenge cold? What had been the catalyst?

The disparity of the cases now made more sense. Total savagery when it came to the men who'd abused her so dreadfully. The social worker who'd not protected her had died in a less brutal fashion. Kate leaned forward, willing Chloe to go faster. Was she right in thinking that Melanie Smith would be the next victim? After all, it sounded as though Melanie had been as much of a victim as Karen herself had...

She's a killer, Kate. She's a soldier. Empathy is not high on her list of personality traits. Sighing, Kate sat back against the seat once more. Chloe glanced over.

"You okay?"

"Yes. I just... I just keep thinking what a dreadful life Karen Black must have had."

Chloe snorted. "That's hardly an excuse for what we think she's done. Plenty of people have awful lives and don't find it necessary to kill anyone."

"*I* know that." Kate thought, with an inner wince, of some of the more unpleasant memories of her childhood.

Chloe glanced over again. "Yeah, well. We both do."

Silence fell as Chloe negotiated the narrow streets of one of the backwaters of Bristol. Kate glanced in the wing mirror to check the black ARU van was following them. She spotted it two cars back and allowed herself a moment of relief.

Out loud, she said to Chloe, "The one thing is, if we're right, and I think we are, why start killing now? Why not before?"

Chloe shrugged. "Your guess is as good as mine. She was probably abroad. Or in prison."

"Mmm." Kate pondered that one. "I'm not sure about prison. Surely that would have come up on the searches?"

"Well—" Chloe broke off as Melanie's street appeared up ahead. "I'm going to pull in up here. We don't want to get too close without the ARU."

Finding a parking space was difficult. Cursing freely, Chloe traversed the block, the van behind them copying their every move. Eventually, Chloe spotted a small private car park that backed onto an office block and swung the car in there.

"We don't want to get clamped," Kate joked, climbing out. Chloe made no response but smiled tensely. Kate knew how she felt. She could feel the adrenaline start to spike within her, her heart rate beginning to gallop. For a moment, she remembered Theo and his wish to be an action hero and smiled. Now she knew what he meant.

Melanie Smith's house was dark and silent, the curtains on the windows drawn. The armed team spread out, quickly and quietly taking up their positions. The supervising officer this time was a good looking dark-haired man in his thirties, who introduced himself as Sergeant Chris Wilde. He, Kate and Chloe stood back from the house, quietly discussing what their plan of action was to be.

"You ready for us to go in?" asked Chris.

"Yes," said Kate. "Tell us when it's safe for us to come in."

"It may not be. We won't know what we're dealing with until we're inside, and these things can escalate very quickly."

Kate nodded and handed him the spare set of keys she'd collected from the housing association that provided Melanie with her accommodation. "You'll be able to go in quietly, at least."

The two women retreated further back down the road, near to where uniformed officers were cordoning off the area. A curious crowd was already beginning to form behind the crime scene tape. Kate swore quietly, wishing that this were happening in the middle of the night so fewer people would be around.

She and Chloe watched as Sergeant Wilde approached the door of the house, one of his officers by his side.

"He's *cute*," said Chloe.

Kate turned to her with a grimace. "Bird! This is not the time." She turned back to see the two officers enter the building with barely a sound, two more men following them. The women waited, tensely.

The silence from the house dragged on and on, broken only by the sounds of the city around them. One of the streetlights above Kate's head was broken, leaving the scene to be lit inadequately by the orange glow of the remaining lights. She realised she was digging her nails into the palms of her hands and forced herself to relax them.

Then there came a fusillade of muffled shouts from inside the flat, a man's voice yelling something that wasn't quite clear. Kate and Chloe flinched. The wind briefly changed and they heard mere words— *where you are—hands above—* before the breeze blew the voice back into unintelligible noise once more.

Kate realised she hadn't breathed for some time and let out her breath in a huff. She heard Chloe do the same behind her.

"No shots," whispered Chloe.

"Don't tempt fate." Kate realised she was quivering

with tension, waiting for the inevitable sound of gunfire. How different it was now to when she started as an officer. She'd gone three years without even *seeing* a gun, whether in the hands of an officer or a suspect.

The blind at one of the windows of the flat suddenly glowed with yellow light. Then there was movement at the door of the flat and Sergeant Wilde emerged. He looked towards the two women and inclined his head in a 'come here' gesture. Kate and Chloe exchanged a glance, perfectly communicating their thoughts in complete silence, and then ran quietly but quickly towards the door.

When they reached him, Chris Wilde leant forward to speak to them in an undertone. "Suspect is in the flat. She doesn't appear to be armed but I'm not taking any chances."

"Have you arrested her?" Kate replied in an equally quite voice.

Chris hesitated. "No—it's... You'll see. Come through, she's under heavy guard." As Chloe stepped forward, he shook his head. "Just one of you. There's no room for more in there, anyway."

Kate squeezed her friend's arm as Chloe obediently stepped back. Swallowing, she followed Chris Wilde's broad back through the poky hallway and ascended the stairs to the room she recognised as Melanie Smith's bedroom. The door was open, painting a stripe of golden light onto the dirty floor of the hallway.

Chris Wilde stepped aside so Kate could see into the room.

The first thing that Kate saw was Melanie Smith, curled like a comma on the floor, her hands tied behind her back with a cable tie. She was so still that for a moment Kate thought she was dead, before she saw the faint rise and fall of her chest and the flutter of a wisp of hair that lay across her half open mouth. The second thing was a woman, sitting on the edge of Melanie's single bed, her hands gripping the duvet. She sat rigid, so still she might have been one of her own statues, staring ahead with unseeing eyes. Kate had a flash of memory; visiting her mother in a psychiatric hospital, one of the other patients there sat like a waxwork in one of the chairs, her eyes fixed on something only she could see. *Catatonic.*

Kate inched into the room. On either side of her, the tall black-clad officers of the ARU kept their weapons trained on Karen Black, who took as much notice of them as she did of Kate—none at all. Kate wondered what she was seeing, what she was remembering, and she swallowed down a rush of stomach acid that hit the back of her throat.

Making very sure she stood out of the firing line of the guns, Kate cleared her throat gently and spoke.

"Karen?" It felt strange, calling her that, remembering how she'd sat opposite her in her sad little office, thinking of her as Rachel Brown.

No response. For a fanciful second, Kate was

convinced the woman had actually *died* and for some reason had stayed sitting upright, rigid even in death.

But, no. Just as with Melanie lying on the floor, Kate could see the rise and fall of Karen's ribcage under the black fleece she wore zipped to the neck. Black trousers, black boots. An assassin's outfit. Kate remembered the baggy dress Karen had been wearing when she had first met her, hiding the muscled body that she could now see under layers of woolly disguise.

She tried again. "Karen? Can you hear me?"

For a moment, all she could hear was the laboured breathing of four sets of male lungs and the thunder of her own heartbeat in her ears.

Then there was a faint sigh. Karen's fixed stare flickered and she blinked a little, as if waking from a deep and nightmare-filled sleep. Her gaze fixed itself to Kate's face.

"What do you want?" Karen asked. Her voice was so oddly measured—so calm—that Kate repressed an involuntary shudder. This woman counselled people, she thought; vulnerable people. It was odd if you thought about it. Why didn't going through a traumatic childhood mean you became more sympathetic to people in similar pain? In Kate's case, it had done. But perhaps for some people it meant they thought along the lines of 'well, I had to go through it so why shouldn't they?'.

All these thoughts went through Kate's mind in

the blink of an eye. Out loud she said, as gently as possible, "I want to know why you did it, Karen."

Karen's face flickered. "You know why," she said, after a moment.

Kate took a deep breath. "Your accusation—why you went to the police station about William Bathford—it was true. Wasn't it?"

"Of course it was. It was the other times, as well. That Barry—he was a teacher, he used to come and give us private lessons. You can guess what he was actually doing." For a moment, Karen's lips drew back in a silent snarl. "Nobody believed me."

Kate, for a moment, couldn't speak. She remembered the news headlines about the other child abuse scandals of the last twenty years, covered up for decades by incompetent social workers, corrupt councils, uncaring police, a culture of victim blaming, of sexualising children. "They should have done," was all she could manage, blinking hard.

Karen must have seen her distress. Her set face softened a little, just a little, but her hands remained where they were, gripping the grubby duvet.

Kate took hold of her emotions. "Why now, Karen? Why did you wait so long for your... for your revenge?"

Karen's gaze slid off to the side. "I was abroad. Australia. I was... I did some time. For a few things."

Kate mentally raised a salute to Chloe, who'd suggested both those possibilities. "So why come back?"

She had almost forgotten the armed men in the room, so focused was she on Karen's face. That face contracted briefly and then hardened again. Karen's gaze met Kate's once more.

"I was raped," Karen said softly.

Kate's intake of breath was echoed by one of the ARU officers. She nodded, slowly, keeping her eyes on Karen. "I'm sorry," was all she said.

Karen half-smiled. "You know," she said, after a moment, "I actually think you are."

Kate took a deep breath. "I *am* sorry. I want to help you."

Karen looked down again. "You can't."

"So, what happens now?"

Karen looked up. A tear tracked its way down her cheek and slid into the black neckline of her fleece. There was a long silence.

"Now it's over," Karen said, almost in a whisper. She looked down at Melanie, lying on the floor. "I was going to kill her. I think I was."

"But you're not now," said Kate; a statement, not a question.

"No, I'm not now," Karen said. Her shoulders sagged and she released her hands from the edge of the bed, spreading trembling fingers.

Kate took another deep breath. "Karen Black, I'm arresting you—"

She got no further. In one swift movement, Karen whipped her hand behind her back and stood up, bringing something forward in one hand that shone in the dim light. Kate barely had time to react before Karen lunged towards her. A millisecond later, she was deafened by gunshots as all four officers opened fire. Karen, hit in the chest and stomach, dropped like a stone to the ground, directly onto the silent still body of Melanie Smith.

Kate stood, rooted to the spot, trembling, her ears ringing. The smell of cordite in the room was acrid, the air hazy. The ARU officers ran forward, and for a moment, all Kate could see was a mass of black-clad bodies bending over the two women on the ground. She opened her mouth to ask the question, but she wasn't able to find the words or her voice.

A strong arm gripped her shoulders from behind, and Chris Wilde's voice said in her still-ringing ear, "With me, DI Redman, if you please. Come back this way with me, nice and slow now."

Kate was grateful for his arm. Her legs were shaking beneath her. He walked her back out into the hallway and into the open air and the night, where Chloe was standing with her hands to her mouth. The moment she saw Kate, she opened her arms and Kate, stumbling forward as Chris released her, fell into them with relief.

Chapter Twenty Nine

"BLOODY *HELL*," WAS THEO'S OPENING remark, the next morning in the office. Rav said nothing but just whistled, his eyebrows raised. "So, she's dead?"

"Of course she's dead," snapped Kate, who was feeling as stretched as if she were made out of rubber. Chloe, sitting beside her, put an arm around her shoulders, and Kate gave her a grateful glance. "She was shot four times. Nobody could have survived it."

"Bloody hell," said Theo, again. "But she had a weapon, right?"

Chloe and Kate exchanged glances. Kate opened her mouth to reply but was prevented by the sound of the door opening. They all looked around to see DCI Weaver entering the room, looking tired.

"Good morning," said Nicola. "I'll make this debrief as quick as possible, I can appreciate we're all exhausted. Kate, how are you?"

"I'm okay, thanks." Kate smiled at her boss, thinking what a change a few months had made. She heard Theo clear his throat and wanted to squeeze his hand in a show of support, but he was standing too far away.

"Right. Good." Nicola became brisk. "Now, as you

no doubt all know by now, our prime suspect Karen Black was apprehended last night at the home of Melanie Smith. She attempted to attack DI Redman and was shot dead by the ARU officers on the spot." She paused and there was a moment of silence. "Naturally, as is usual with the death of the suspect in custody, there will be an internal investigation, but I don't think we or indeed Chris Wilde and his team have anything to worry about. The subject was armed, after all."

Kate raised an arm. "May I say something?"

Nicola looked surprised, but inclined her head in acquiescence. "Go on, Kate."

"I'm sorry, I haven't had a chance to tell you yet."

Nicola frowned. "That's okay. Please go on."

Kate lowered her arm and glanced about the room. She sighed before speaking. "She wasn't armed."

Chloe, who knew what had happened, was the only person not to react.

Theo said "*What*?"

"That's not the impression I had from my conversation with Sergeant Wilde," said Nicola, her frown deepening.

Kate reached for her phone and brought up her picture gallery, flicking to the photographs she'd taken late last night. She held up her phone so that everyone could see it. "This is the only thing she was armed with."

They all crowded round to look. Rav gasped.

"That's a toy gun," said Theo, blankly.

"Yes." That was all Kate could say, for the moment.

"May I?" Nicola took the phone from Kate's hand and brought it closer to her face. "So it is. Just a plastic toy gun." She handed the phone back to Kate. "Why, I wonder? Bluffing? Madness?"

Kate put her phone back in her handbag. "I think... I think she wanted to die." She thought back to the single tear sliding down Karen's cheek just before it happened, a liquid trail of gold in the warm lamp light. "A soldier's death. A certain, quick death."

Chloe nodded. She put her arm around Kate's shoulders again. "I think so too. Death by firing squad, as it were."

"Well..." That was all Nicola said, softly.

There was a moment of silence while they all contemplated the fact. Then, Nicola stepped back over to the whiteboards and scanned them, taking in the victims and the suspects. But who were the real victims, thought Kate. *Who* were *the real victims?*

Nicola turned back, clearing her throat. "I do have one more thing to say before I dismiss you."

They all listened expectedly. Nicola, turning slightly pinker than normal, went on. "I've taken up the offer of a transfer—a promotion, in fact. I'll be moving over to Bristol CID. Over the next six weeks, obviously we'll be interviewing for my successor."

Kate felt her eyebrows shoot up. She didn't dare

look across at Theo. Or perhaps this wasn't a surprise for him?

It was funny; six months ago, the news of Nicola's departure would have had her cheering, but now... Now Kate almost felt sorry about it. Her relationship with her boss had changed so much for the better. Oh well, it was Nicola's choice. Kate focused her attention back on what DCI Weaver was saying.

"—wanted to thank you all for your hard work on this. It's not been the easiest of cases and I, for one, appreciate the effort that you've all put in."

Nicola's eyes met Kate's and she smiled, properly. Touched and pleased, Kate smiled back.

***

LATER THAT DAY, KATE DROVE to Anderton's cottage, a decent bottle of red wine rolling gently on the car seat beside her. The sun was setting in a blaze of orange and gold cloud and the last remnants of the autumn leaves on the trees fluttered in the gentle breeze. Kate parked her car next to Anderton's in his driveway and hurried towards the door of his cottage, clutching her wine bottle and shivering. The meagre warmth of the sun was rapidly fading as the autumn night took hold.

Anderton opened the door and kissed her. "What a day you must have had."

"It's over now." Kate stepped gratefully into the

warmth of his house and put her arms around him. "I'm home now."

"Yes, you are." Anderton tipped her face up to his and regarded her. "You are home."

There was a moment of silence while they looked at each other, hearing the words that weren't being said.

"Come on in," said Anderton. "I've made up a fire. Come and sit by it with me and we'll talk about the future."

"I'd like that," said Kate. She took his hand, and they walked into the sitting room together.

THE END

ENJOYED THIS BOOK? AN HONEST review left at Amazon and Goodreads is always welcome and *really* important for indie authors. The more reviews an independently published book has, the easier it is to market it and find new readers.

You can leave a review at Amazon US here or Amazon UK here.

Want some more of Celina Grace's work for free? Subscribers to her mailing list get a free digital copy of **Requiem (A Kate Redman Mystery: Book 2)**, a free digital copy of **A Prescription for Death (The Asharton Manor Mysteries Book 2)** *and* a free PDF copy of her short story collection **A Blessing From The Obeah Man.**

Requiem
(A Kate Redman Mystery: Book 2)

WHEN THE BODY OF TROUBLED teenager Elodie Duncan is pulled from the river in Abbeyford, the case is at first assumed to be a straightforward suicide. Detective Sergeant Kate Redman is shocked to discover that she'd met the victim the night before her death, introduced by Kate's younger brother Jay. As the case develops, it becomes clear that Elodie was murdered. A talented young musician, Elodie had been keeping some strange company and was hiding her own dark secrets.

As the list of suspects begin to grow, so do the questions. What is the significance of the painting Elodie modelled for? Who is the man who was seen with her on the night of her death? Is there any connection with another student's death at the exclusive musical college that Elodie attended?

As Kate and her partner Detective Sergeant Mark Olbeck attempt to unravel the mystery, the dark undercurrents of the case threaten those whom Kate holds most dear...

A Prescription For Death (The Asharton Manor Mysteries: Book 2) – A Novella

"I HAD A SURGE OF kinship the first time I saw the manor, perhaps because we'd both seen better days."

It is 1947. Asharton Manor, once one of the most beautiful stately homes in the West Country, is now a convalescent home for former soldiers. Escaping the devastation of post-war London is Vivian Holt, who moves to the nearby village and begins to volunteer as a nurse's aide at the manor. Mourning the death of her soldier husband, Vivian finds solace in her new friendship with one of the older patients, Norman Winter, someone who has served his country in both world wars. Slowly, Vivian's heart begins to heal, only to be torn apart when she arrives for work one day to be told that Norman is dead.

It seems a straightforward death, but is it? Why did a particular photograph disappear from Norman's possessions after his death? Who is the sinister figure who keeps following Vivian? Suspicion and doubts begin to grow and when another death occurs, Vivian begins to realise that the war may be over but the real battle is just beginning...

A Blessing From The Obeah Man

DARE YOU READ ON? HORRIFYING, scary, sad and thought-provoking, this short story collection will take you on a macabre journey. In the titular story, a honeymooning couple take a wrong turn on their trip around Barbados. The Mourning After brings you a shivery story from a suicidal teenager. In Freedom Fighter, an unhappy middle-aged man chooses the wrong day to make a bid for freedom, whereas Little Drops of Happiness and Wave Goodbye are tales of darkness from sunny Down Under. Strapping Lass and The Club are for those who prefer, shall we say, a little meat to the story...

JUST GO TO CELINA'S WEBSITE to sign up. It's quick, easy and free. Be the first to be informed of promotions, giveaways, new releases and subscriber-only benefits by subscribing to her (occasional) newsletter.

Aspiring or new authors might like to check out Celina's other site http://www.indieauthorschool. com for motivation, inspiration and advice on writing and publishing a book, or even starting a whole new career as an indie author. Get a free eBook, a mini e-course, cheat sheets and other helpful downloads when you sign up for the newsletter.

http://www.celinagrace.com

http://www.indieauthorschool.com

Twitter:
@celina__grace

Facebook:
http://www.facebook.com/authorcelinagrace

More Books By Celina Grace...

Hushabye
(A Kate Redman Mystery: Book 1)

ON THE FIRST DAY OF her new job in the West Country, Detective Sergeant Kate Redman finds herself investigating the kidnapping of Charlie Fullman, the newborn son of a wealthy entrepreneur and his trophy wife. It seems a straightforward case... but as Kate and her fellow officer Mark Olbeck delve deeper, they uncover murky secrets and multiple motives for the crime.

Kate finds the case bringing up painful memories of her own past secrets. As she confronts the truth about herself, her increasing emotional instability threatens both her hard-won career success and the possibility that they will ever find Charlie Fullman alive...

Hushabye is the book that introduces
Detective Sergeant Kate Redman.
Available from Amazon Kindle.

Imago
(A Kate Redman Mystery: Book 3)

"THEY DON'T FEAR ME, QUITE the opposite. It makes it twice as fun... I know the next time will be soon, I've learnt to recognise the signs. I think I even know who it will be. She's oblivious of course, just as she should be. All the time, I watch and wait and she has no idea, none at all. And why would she? I'm disguised as myself, the very best disguise there is."

A known prostitute is found stabbed to death in a shabby corner of Abbeyford. Detective Sergeant Kate Redman and her partner Detective Sergeant Olbeck take on the case, expecting to have it wrapped up in a matter of days. Kate finds herself distracted by her growing attraction to her boss, Detective Chief Inspector Anderton – until another woman's body is found, with the same knife wounds. And then another one after that, in a matter of days.

Forced to confront the horrifying realisation that a serial killer may be preying on the vulnerable women of Abbeyford, Kate, Olbeck and the team find themselves in a race against time to unmask a terrifying murderer, who just might be hiding in plain sight...

Buy Imago on Amazon, available now.

Snarl
(A Kate Redman Mystery: Book 4)

A RESEARCH LABORATORY OPENS ON the outskirts of Abbeyford, bringing with it new people, jobs, prosperity and publicity to the area – as well as a mob of protesters and animal rights activists. The team at Abbeyford police station take this new level of civil disorder in their stride – until a fatal car bombing of one of the laboratory's head scientists means more drastic measures must be taken...

Detective Sergeant Kate Redman is struggling to come to terms with being back at work after long period of absence on sick leave; not to mention the fact that her erstwhile partner Olbeck has now been promoted above her. The stakes get even higher as a multiple murder scene is uncovered and a violent activist is implicated in the crime. Kate and the team must put their lives on the line to expose the murderer and untangle the snarl of accusations, suspicions and motives.

Available now from Amazon.

Chimera
(A Kate Redman Mystery: Book 5)

THE WEST COUNTRY TOWN OF Abbeyford is celebrating its annual pagan festival, when the festivities are interrupted by the discovery of a very decomposed body. Soon, several other bodies are discovered but is it a question of foul play or are these deaths from natural causes?

It's a puzzle that Detective Sergeant Kate Redman and the team could do without, caught up as they are in investigating an unusual series of robberies. Newly single again, Kate also has to cope with her upcoming Inspector exams and a startling announcement from her friend and colleague DI Mark Olbeck...

When a robbery goes horribly wrong, Kate begins to realise that the two cases might be linked. She must use all her experience and intelligence to solve a serious of truly baffling crimes which bring her up against an old adversary from her past...

Buy Chimera (A Kate Redman Mystery: Book 5) from Amazon, available now.

Echo
(A Kate Redman Mystery: Book 6)

THE WEST COUNTRY TOWN OF Abbeyford is suffering its worst floods in living memory when a landslide reveals the skeletal remains of a young woman. Detective Sergeant Kate Redman is assigned to the case but finds herself up against a baffling lack of evidence, missing files and the suspicion that someone on high is blocking her investigation...

Matters are complicated by her estranged mother making contact after years of silence. As age-old secrets are uncovered and powerful people are implicated, Kate and the team are determined to see justice done. But at what price?

Now available from Amazon.

Creed
(A Kate Redman Mystery: Book 7)

JOSHUA WIDCOMBE AND KAYA TRENT were the golden couple of Abbeyford's School of Art and Drama; good-looking, popular and from loving, stable families. So why did they kill themselves on the grassy stage of the college's outdoor theatre?

Detective Chief Inspector Anderton thinks there might be something more to the case than a straightforward teenage suicide pact. Detective Sergeant Kate Redman agrees with him, but nothing is certain until another teenager at the college kills herself, quickly followed by yet another death. Why are the privileged teens of this exclusive college killing themselves? Is this a suicide cluster?

As Kate and the team delve deeper into the case, secrets and lies rear their ugly heads and Abbeyford CID are about to find out that sometimes, the most vulnerable people can be the most deadly...

Available now from Amazon.

Sanctuary
(A Kate Redman Mystery: Book 8)

DAWN BREAKS AT MUDDIFORD BEACH and the body of a young African man is discovered lying on the sand. Was he a desperate asylum seeker, drowned in his attempt to reach the safe shores of Britain? Or is there a more sinister explanation for his death?

Irritated to discover that the investigation will be a joint one with the neighbouring police force at Salterton CID, Detective Sergeant Kate Redman is further annoyed by her Salterton counterpart, one of the rudest young women Kate has ever encountered.

Tensions rise as the two teams investigate the case and when a second body is discovered, Kate and her colleagues are to about realise just how far people will go in the cause of doing good...

Available now from Amazon.

Valentine
(A Kate Redman Mystery Novella)

A RESPECTABLE, MIDDLE-AGED HOUSEWIFE. AN ambitious young lawyer. A student burlesque dancer. Three women with nothing in common – except for the fact that someone has sent them a macabre Valentine's Day gift; a pig's heart pierced by an arrow.

Is this a case of serious harm intended? Or just a malicious prank? Detective Inspector Olbeck thinks there might be something more sinister behind it but his colleague Detective Sergeant Kate Redman is too busy mourning the departure of her partner Tin to New York to worry too much about the case. Until one of the women receives a death threat...

Available now from Amazon.

Interested in historical mysteries?

The Asharton Manor Mysteries

SOME OLD HOUSES HAVE MORE history than others...
The Asharton Manor Mysteries Boxed Set is a four part series of novellas spanning the twentieth century. Each standalone story (about 20,000 words) uses Asharton Manor as the backdrop to a devious and twisting crime mystery. The boxed set includes the following stories:

Death at the Manor

IT IS 1929. ASHARTON MANOR stands alone in the middle of a pine forest, once the place where ancient pagan ceremonies were undertaken in honour of the goddess Astarte. The Manor is one of the most beautiful stately homes in the West Country and seems like a palace to Joan Hart, newly arrived from London to take up a servant's position as the head kitchen maid. Getting to grips with her new role and with her fellow workers, Joan is kept busy, but not too busy to notice that the glittering surface of life at the Manor might be hiding some dark secrets. The beautiful and wealthy mistress of the house, Delphine Denford, keeps falling ill but why? Confiding her thoughts to her friend and fellow housemaid Verity Hunter, Joan is unsure of what exactly is making her uneasy, but then Delphine Denford dies... Armed only with their own good sense and quick thinking, Joan and Verity must pit their wits against a cunning murderer in order to bring them to justice.

A Prescription for Death

IT IS 1947. ASHARTON MANOR, once one of the most beautiful stately homes in the West Country, is now a convalescent home for former soldiers. Escaping the devastation of post-war London is Vivian Holt, who moves to the nearby village and begins to volunteer as a nurse's aide at the manor. Mourning the death of her soldier husband, Vivian finds solace in her new friendship with one of the older patients, Norman Winter, someone who has served his country in both world wars. Slowly, Vivian's heart begins to heal, only to be torn apart when she arrives for work one day to be told that Norman is dead. It seems a straightforward death, but is it? Why did a particular photograph disappear from Norman's possessions after his death? Who is the sinister figure who keeps following Vivian? Suspicion and doubts begin to grow and when another death occurs, Vivian begins to realise that the war may be over but the real battle is just beginning...

The Rhythm of Murder

IT IS 1973. EVE AND Janey, two young university students, are en route to a Bristol commune when they take an unexpected detour to the little village of Midford. Seduced by the roguish charms of a young man who picks them up in the village pub, they are astonished to find themselves at Asharton Manor, now the residence of the very wealthy, very famous, very degenerate Blue Turner, lead singer of rock band Dirty Rumours. The golden summer rolls on, full of sex, drugs and rock and roll, but Eve begins to sense that there may be a sinister side to all the hedonism. And then one day, Janey disappears, seemingly run away... but as Eve begins to question what happened to her friend, she realises that she herself might be in terrible danger...

Number Thirteen, Manor Close

IT IS 2014. BEATRICE AND Mike Dunhill are finally moving into a house of their own, Number Thirteen, Manor Close. Part of the brand new Asharton Estate, Number Thirteen is built on the remains of the original Asharton Manor which was destroyed in a fire in 1973. Still struggling a little from the recent death of her mother, Beatrice is happy to finally have a home of her own – until she begins to experience some strange happenings that, try as she might, she can't explain away. Her husband Mike seems unconvinced and only her next door neighbour Mia seems to understand Beatrice's growing fear of her home. Uncertain of her own judgement, Beatrice must confront what lies beneath the beautiful surface of the Asharton Estate. But can she do so without losing her mind – or her life?

CELINA GRACE'S PSYCHOLOGICAL THRILLER, **LOST Girls** is also available from Amazon:

Twenty-three years ago, Maudie Sampson's childhood friend Jessica disappeared on a family holiday in Cornwall. She was never seen again.

In the present day, Maudie is struggling to come to terms with the death of her wealthy father, her increasingly fragile mental health and a marriage that's under strain. Slowly, she becomes aware that there is someone following her: a blonde woman in a long black coat with an intense gaze. As the woman begins to infiltrate her life, Maudie realises no one else appears to be able to see her.

Is Maudie losing her mind? Is the woman a figment of her imagination or does she actually exist? Have the sins of the past caught up with Maudie's present... or is there something even more sinister going on?

Lost Girls is a novel from the author of **The House on Fever Street**: a dark and convoluted tale which proves that nothing can be taken for granted and no-one is as they seem.

Currently available on Amazon

THE HOUSE ON FEVER STREET is the first psychological thriller by **Celina Grace**.

Thrown together in the aftermath of the London bombings of 2005, Jake and Bella embark on a passionate and intense romance. Soon Bella is living with Jake in his house on Fever Street, along with his sardonic brother Carl and Carl's girlfriend, the beautiful but chilly Veronica.

As Bella tries to come to terms with her traumatic experience, her relationship with Jake also becomes a source of unease. Why do the housemates never go into the garden? Why does Jake have such bad dreams and such explosive outbursts of temper?

Bella is determined to understand the man she loves but as she uncovers long-buried secrets, is she putting herself back into mortal danger?

The House on Fever Street is the first psychological thriller from writer Celina Grace - a chilling study of the violent impulses that lurk beneath the surfaces of everyday life.

Shortlisted for the 2006 Crime Writers' Association Debut Dagger Award.

Currently available on Amazon

Acknowledgements

Many thanks to all the following splendid souls:

Chris Howard for the brilliant cover designs; Andrea Harding for editing and proofreading; lifelong Schlockers and friends David Hall, Ben Robinson and Alberto Lopez; Ross McConnell for advice on police procedural and for also being a great brother; Kathleen and Pat McConnell, Anthony Alcock, Naomi White, Mo Argyle, Lee Benjamin, Bonnie Wede, Sherry and Amali Stoute, Cheryl and Mark Beckles, Georgia Lucas-Going, Steven Lucas, Loletha Stoute and Harry Lucas, Helen Parfect, Helen Watson, Emily Way, Sandy Hall, Kristýna Vosecká and of course my lovely Mabel, Jethro and Isaiah.

Printed in Great Britain
by Amazon